FIRE WITHIN

AMY KNUPP

FIRE WITHIN

S ophie Alexander was going to die alone.

While she had long ago made the choice to *live* by herself, to be independent and self-sufficient in every way, dying alone was different. Creepy. Unnerving.

Okay, terrifying.

She was in her office — she knew that much. But everything else was confusing, including the layout, which she'd thought she knew back and forth and upside down. She should, as much time as she spent here. But the heat and the thick, lung-scorching smoke had sent her internal GPS powers to hell. Plus, the throbbing, swelling knot on the side of her head hurt so badly she couldn't think straight.

Ironic that her life's mission was to make the world greener, safer, and she was going to be asphyxiated by vile, poisonous gases in a fire.

Irony could suck it.

Her mind was scrambled like an egg, like the frog her satanspawn brother had run through their mother's good blender when he was thirteen. No. She was not going to waste a single thought on him, especially if these were among her last.

And she was definitely not going to just lie here and give up. Giving up went against everything inside of her. She'd never been a quitter, and lying in a stifling, smoke-filled sweatbox, coughing her brains out, was not going to change that.

She didn't want to die. She had too much to live for. She had a company to run, buildings to improve, personal goals to kick ass at, literally and figuratively. Lying here and giving up was not an option.

Sophie pulled her smoke-saturated shirt over her mouth and nose, as if that would help much, and fought hard to stop coughing with every inhale. She hoisted her concrete-heavy body up on all fours as best she could and crawled a few feet, unsure of the direction she moved in but thinking if she kept going, she'd eventually run in to something. Preferably an exit.

Heavy, blinding smoke was a bitch. One of the worst parts of being a firefighter, in Nate Rottinghaus's opinion. Masks were a pain in the ass, but he couldn't imagine doing the job without one, the way they had just a couple decades ago. He adjusted his again, praying his supply would last.

He was deep inside the second level of the two-story office building, crawling as low to the floor as he could get. Visibility: zero. Status quo. He continued to navigate by touch, blindly searching every inch in front of him with his gloved hands. Hoping.

One of the tenants from the first floor of the building, who hadn't been present when the fire had broken out, reported that the tenant in the upstairs office on the north end — this one — might be inside. A thirty-something female who practically lived in her office. Her Lexus SUV was in the lot, and the downstairs tenant had heard her footsteps above his office just a couple of hours ago. No one had seen her leave.

Nate was all business when he was working a fire. Couldn't afford not to be. Two years ago, he'd learned the up-close-and-personal way that lives could be altered in a millisecond in the heart of a blaze. Thank God for Faith Mendoza, his former colleague and now the chief's wife, who'd saved his sorry ass.

Nate was still waiting for his opportunity to pay it forward.

As the minutes ticked by, his adrenaline pumped even harder. She had to be in here somewhere. His optimism had soared when he'd located a couch, thinking maybe she'd fallen asleep there, but there was no one on it or near it, and now time was running out. His air supply must be close to empty — he expected to get the five-minute warning vibration any second. But he couldn't quit until he ran into Evan Drake, his colleague who'd gone left when Nate had gone right, in the middle. Until they found the woman or verified there was nobody inside.

Keep it together, he told himself. *Gotta be getting close.*

A few seconds later, his left hand ran into something soft, pliable. A foot?

Pulling himself along by the elbows, he scooted closer and took his left glove off with his teeth. A leg, he verified as he groped his way over a muscled calf, a knee, a thigh. A short leg. Feminine. He thought he heard a moan, but it was hard to tell, between all his gear and the sounds of the others actively fighting the blaze about twenty feet to the south. Too damn close.

He eased himself alongside her and fumbled around for his flashlight, breaking out in a sudden sweat that had nothing to do with the hundred-plus-degree heat in here.

People depended on him to be a professional and to keep his shit together, in every way, when he was inside a burning building. Doubly so when there was a life at stake. Normally, he was cool under pressure. Able to think straight about whatever situation was at hand. Systematic. Practical. Experienced.

So when he shined his light into this woman's face, it defied all logic and acceptability that the first thing that went through his mind was that she had the most compelling brown eyes he'd ever seen.

The second was that those eyes were staring back at him with a certain measure of awareness. Relief. She was conscious, if disoriented. Scared as hell, understandably. The urge erupted in him to assuage that fear, to put his arms around her and reassure her — on a personal level. And that was messed up.

Those were some powerful eyes.

Nate grabbed his radio and reported in: "Female victim located. Conscious. Bringing her out."

He propelled himself the last few inches until he was even with her head, taking a final deep pull on his air supply. "Everything's gonna be okay," he told the woman as he pulled his mask from his face and opened himself up to the chemical-laden smoky air. She responded only with a wicked cough. She'd no doubt taken in a shit-ton of the potentially deadly air. Nate eased the mask over her nose and mouth, standard operating procedures be damned, coaching her to get some of the purified air into her system, which he knew was easier said than done in her apparent condition. Time to get her the hell out of here *stat*.

"Can you walk with me?" he asked next to her ear.

The woman coughed repeatedly as she tried to inhale from the mask … but she nodded.

He frowned, not convinced. "Let's give it a try. Stay low."

They made it three steps before her coughing and wheezing overtook her.

"I'm going to help you," he said, leaning close. He thought he saw a minute nod, but he didn't spare the time to analyze.

He hoped like hell she didn't have any unseen injuries as he hoisted her into his arms. She weighed next to nothing; if he hadn't looked into her eyes, he'd think she was a child by her size.

The smoke was already burning the inside of his nose and all the way down his air passages into his lungs. Which meant the vic must be in a hell of a lot of pain.

Nate kept as low as possible, focused on finding the most direct way back out — not an easy task when he had crawled methodically back and forth over every inch of space looking for her, the smoke messing with his orientation, and couldn't see two inches in front of his face. He suspected — hoped — the door was about fifteen feet ahead, on the other side of the couch.

The woman tightened her death squeeze on his neck with surprising strength, which was a good sign. Her will to survive was strong. She was likely going to need that in spades once he got her out of here into the paramedics' hands.

As he made his way around another piece of furniture, something popped in front of his face and would've drawn a curse from him had he had oxygen to waste on it. A split second later, he realized it was his mask. She was offering him a fresh breath. His heart pounded in gratitude that was probably less than heroic, and he held it to his face, not stopping their slow progress as he sucked in one long breath of clean air. The very second his lungs were full, the low-air warning beep went off. Five minutes left on his supply. He paused long enough to make sure the mask was over the woman's face again and then set off, knowing they had to be close to the place he'd entered, trusting his instincts, praying they were right and he wouldn't let this woman down.

They made it out in less than four minutes — the most excruciating four minutes of Nate's life. Rafe and Niko, two of the paramedics, were waiting with a stretcher a few feet from the building. Nate paused in front of it, looked down into those brown eyes that seemed to implore him not to desert her. For a crazy second, he didn't want to let her go.

"Rottinghaus?" Rafe shouted loudly enough to be heard over the racket.

It was enough to snap him out of his stupor.

"These guys are the best medics you could have," he told the woman. "They'll take good care of you."

He lowered her to the stretcher, and they rushed her off before he could say another word.

Paige Hegel, another of the EMS team, hurried over to Nate and tried to usher him toward another ambulance.

"I'm fine," he said, fighting not to cough, knowing it wouldn't take much to get sent off to the hospital. "Just need to catch my breath."

Chief Joe Mendoza approached with concern and purpose blazing from his eyes. He gestured to Nate and then to the ambulance, yelling something Nate couldn't hear over all the commotion.

"He said you need to be checked," Paige shouted, even though she was right next to him, her arm looped around his.

Nate opened his mouth to tell her what he thought of that, and damn if he didn't start coughing.

He spotted a group around the brown-eyed woman he'd carried out, next to the first ambulance in line, and decided allowing Paige to smack some O2 on him would give him the chance to see how she was faring, check to see if she was still conscious or if her condition had worsened. He only wanted to check because she was his first rescue ever. Professional concern.

As Paige sat him down, hooked him up with a mask, and checked his vitals, he helplessly watched the paramedics work on the nameless woman about twenty feet away. He could only see the top of her dark head. Couldn't tell whether she was moving or not.

His heart hammered, and he tried to convince himself it was just the rescue and the adrenaline rush that went with it. But as they loaded her in the box, their frantic pace telling him that every second was crucial, all he could see in his mind were those beautiful, terrified, determined eyes.

2

The next day, Nate made it almost three hours lying to himself after his shift ended at seven a.m. Telling himself he wasn't going to check on the woman he'd helped out of the fire. Pretending he could get those brown eyes out of his mind.

Sophie Alexander. Age thirty-one. Owner of Green Systems Inc. That was the lump sum of the info he'd managed to glean between the time the crew had returned to the station after the fire and now. Not nearly enough. He was compelled to find out everything about her.

Dude, you sound like a psychopath or a stalker. Rein it in.

He entered the main door of the hospital instead of going through the ER department he was much more familiar with. No reason to call attention to the fact that he was visiting a woman he didn't know. Sure, he'd heard of guys following up on the victims they rescued, but... He was afraid maybe he was *too* interested in seeing Sophie again. Nothing going on inside of him felt normal or acceptable. The need to see her again made no sense, at least not to the extent he felt it, and it meant one of two things: either he was acting like an overenthusiastic rookie about his first rescue, which wasn't cool at all, especially for a guy who'd been fighting fires for fourteen years, or he had half a raging crush on a woman he'd never even had a conversation with before, which was, well … weird.

At the info desk, Nate whipped out his badge and flashed it at the fragile-looking but eager volunteer manning it, a woman who looked to be in her eighties. "I rescued a young woman from a fire last night and was wondering if you could give me her room number so I can check on her."

The woman grinned warmly, as he'd expected. "I certainly can. Her name?"

Once he had the information he needed, he headed up to the third floor, wondering how many of Sophie's family members and friends he'd have to reckon with. If her room was crowded, he'd just poke his head in, reassure himself that Sophie was okay, and get the hell out.

He needn't have worried about it. Sophie's room was empty of visitors.

He was momentarily stunned by that revelation, and it took him a good three seconds to focus on Sophie's face and realize she was out cold. He backed out of the room, alarmed. Had she lost consciousness and failed to come to yet? He hadn't had a clear view of her at the scene, only of the people surrounding her, working on her. How serious was her condition? Smoke inhalation could be damn serious, but he'd assumed her case wasn't critical based on the sole fact that she'd been conscious when he'd gotten her out of the building.

Moronic assumption on his part.

When he was nearly to the nurse's station to inquire, he stopped.

Dumb ass. If she weren't conscious, she'd likely be in ICU.

The lone nurse at the station, a brunette wearing scrubs with cartoon frogs all over them, looked up at him and smiled. "Hel-looo," she purred. "Something I can help you with?"

Nate flashed a smile and shook his head, then backed away. He returned to Sophie's room, more confident that she was only napping.

He stopped a couple of feet from her bed and stared, finally taking in the sight of her, the details he'd missed when he'd flipped out before. The bed dwarfed her, and the white sheets somehow made her skin look even paler. She was connected to oxygen and monitors and hadn't moved a muscle since he'd barged into her room the first time, as far as he could tell.

Her head was propped up about thirty degrees, and the blankets hit her mid-chest, revealing a stiff-looking mint-green hospital gown that did nothing for her complexion. Sophie's dark, shoulder-length hair was a mess, sticking every which way on her head, fanning out on the pillow.

And yet his heart pounded.

He shook his head against the reaction. Sauntered toward the large window that would likely show a distant view of San Amaro Island if there weren't layers of buildings in the way. It was only a half thought, though, as his mind and his gaze veered back to Sophie Alexander.

She hadn't stirred, and he should probably get the hell out of here, give her some privacy. Get some sleep himself, as he'd been up for going on thirty hours now, with the exception of finally drifting off about thirty minutes before he'd had to wake up at the station this morning. Maybe sleep would cure the fucked-up compulsion in him to touch this woman, to pull her into his chest and protect her from further harm.

Fucked. Up.

He turned to walk out. Made it almost to the door but then stopped, the need to check one more time whether her eyes were open too overwhelming to ignore.

They weren't.

The modest-sized room swallowed her up, and Nate couldn't stand the idea of her waking up all alone. He picked up a wood-framed vinyl chair from the wall, set it down at the foot of her bed, and settled into it to wait.

Awareness licked at Sophie's mind. Pain. Her head ached, and her throat burned like it was on fire.

Fire. The memory bounced around her brain, expanding to

take up all the space. An acrid bitterness filled her mouth, her nostrils. Seemed to permeate all the way down to every organ inside of her.

She'd been in a fire. Could've died in a fire. An image of thick smoke made her heart lurch in fear.

Panicking, she forced her weighted eyelids open and, without moving her head — because *shit*, it hurt — she drank in details, urging her brain to work. No smoke. Only a memory. White ceiling above intersecting with a pale yellow wall opposite her. A sleek, flat-screen TV was bolted up high, angled downward toward her bed. Something tickled her upper lip, and when she tried to scratch it, her fingers ran into a tube. Oxygen, she remembered.

She tried to breathe in to comfort herself, but air in her throat … it hurt like someone was scraping her windpipe with needles all the way down.

"Sophie?" A deep, soothing, baritone voice from near her feet startled her. As she turned her head toward it, a face popped into her blurry-edged vision.

His face. The one who'd helped her.

Hazel eyes, almost amber-colored, peered down at her beneath creases of worry on his forehead. His short hair was the color of pecans — not blond, not quite brown, with a hint of auburn around the edges — and his facial scruff was long enough to appear soft instead of bristly.

She felt discombobulated, as if she were living in a slow-motion cartoon. Everything was fuzzy, her senses sending weak signals, but she remembered this man had saved her life.

"How you feeling, Sophie?"

She clung to the smoothness of his voice, like warm, melty caramel spreading around her, comforting her. Giving her empty mind something solid to hold on to.

Her attempt to speak failed. She opened her mouth to request a drink, but no sound came out. Swallowing around the desert-dry rawness in her throat made her eyes water at the stab of red-hot pain, and she vowed not to do that again. She pressed a hand to her neck, expecting to feel exterior damage, so painful was the inside passageway, but her fingers found only smooth, clammy flesh. Clearing her throat would likely make speaking possible, but hell no, she wasn't about to try that — not when air rubbed like broken glass through it.

"Water," she whispered, squeezing her eyes shut against the pain that came with the attempt.

"I'll get you a drink," the man said, and gratitude became a tangible warmth in her chest.

She heard his footsteps, three of them. When the footsteps brought him back to her side, she opened her eyes and found him holding a powder-blue plastic cup with a straw sticking out. She tried to sit up.

"You don't need to move," he said, directing the straw to her mouth, the cup to the side of her head. "I've got it. Just drink."

She sucked the room-temperature liquid into her mouth and let it wash over the parched tissue inside, swishing it gently around until every last cell was damp. Then she clamped her eyes shut again and gripped a wad of the bedsheet as she willed the water down her raw throat. She thought she remembered a red-haired nurse telling her to call if the pain meds wore off, but she had no idea whether this level of pain was with or without medical relief. All she knew was it hurt.

"Bet that hurts like crazy," the man said, and she focused on the hint of a Texas drawl in his voice, trying to distract herself from the pain.

Sophie nodded slowly and took the straw in her mouth because the water also soothed.

Five slow swallows was her limit, and when the guy offered her more, she shook her head. He set the cup to the side and returned his attention to her face.

"Thanks," Sophie managed. The sound that came out was low and hoarse. Rough like sharp gravel.

"Don't talk right now, Sophie."

She nodded, frustrated by her inability to let him know her gratitude.

He'd dragged his chair close to her shoulders as he'd held the water, and now he braced one hand on her mattress as he watched her. Sophie touched the back of his hand, trying to convey her thanks. He took her hand in his, his fingers warm and calloused. Gentle.

"Sleep some more," he said in a voice barely above a whisper. "It's gonna hurt for some time. Best to sleep it off if you can. Help your body heal."

"Are you…" She cringed at the burn in her throat. "Staying?"

"I'll be here for a while. Close your eyes."

Her eyes fluttered shut, so heavy, her mind too tired to make sense of anything. Content to hold on to the picture of this man as his finger caressed back and forth over her hand. Soothing. Lulling.

As her brain flitted between consciousness and blessed sleep, she became aware of him shifting, his grip on her hand tightening slightly. Eyes still closed, she felt him leaning closer, and then his warm, moist lips brushed against her forehead. She didn't open her eyes, didn't allow herself to question his touch or to feel awkward. Instead, she succumbed to relief and gratitude and let herself get swept away in the comfort of being … not alone.

3

Dozing in a hospital chair on and off for a few hours wasn't Nate's idea of a good night's sleep … or even a decent nap. There was a distinct kink in his neck from the way his head had dipped to the side. His eyes felt like someone had poured sand over them and he couldn't get the last grains out, and his throat was just about as rough. Sophie's must hurt like a mother. He didn't regret for a second letting her use his air supply.

She'd still been out when he'd finally decided his sitting there in her room for hours on end had crossed over into the creepy zone. He wanted her to know she wasn't alone, but it'd be better if it was a family member camping out and not some single dude who'd been struck stupid by her mesmerizing eyes.

Shit. He was even thinking poetically now. Chalk that up to the lack of sleep.

He'd done what he could, which hadn't been jack shit other than sitting there snoozing and wearing out his welcome. He'd decided on his way out of the hospital that that was it. He'd been there for her, she'd known he was there, and now it was time to move on.

It was after five p.m. His dad was going on a date tonight, so the house would be empty. Of people and of food. Nate drove his Ford F-150 toward the gulf shore and parked in the lot of the

15

Shell Shack. As home-away-from-home as a place without a bed could get.

As he got out of the truck, the life-affirming aroma of fried food and the din of good souls imbibing welcomed him. The patio adjacent to the thatched-roof bar was nearly deserted. Such was November on the beach. Today was particularly windy, and the indoor heaters were the only way to go.

Nate walked through the open doorway, glad to see the protective plastic over the windows on the far side of the open-air shack, blocking the wind coming off the beach.

"Rotten House, get your ass over here!"

Nate turned his head in response to one of his nicknames at the station. Dylan Long sat on the end stool on the far side of the bar, watching him and grinning like a dumb ass. Nate made his way over and took the empty seat next to him.

"Man of the hour," Dylan said and slapped him on the back. "Order up, hero. Dinner's on me."

Jess, their favorite short, curvy waitress, flipped a towel over her shoulder and smiled at him. "Hey, Nate. Heard you're a hero. Way to go."

"Long time coming," he said modestly. He'd heard other guys say they didn't feel heroic after pulling somebody out of a fire, and now he understood. All he'd been doing was his job. Rescues were more about luck … finding someone who needed help before it was too late. Being in the right place at the right time. He just thanked Jesus, Mary, and all that was holy that it hadn't been too late for Sophie.

"Beer's on the house," Jess said, "and I'd suggest a triple burger and a couple of sides if Dylan's got your dinner tab."

Nate smirked at Dylan, then nodded at Jess. "I like the way you think. Triple with cheese and a double order of chili fries, please."

"Dos Equis draw?" Jess asked.

Nate nodded again and stole an onion ring from Dylan. "You the only one here from the station?"

"Clay and Evan said they might show up later. Couple medics were here when I came in, but they left."

"The Shack would probably close down during the winter without the fire department," Jess said as she slid a glass of amber liquid perfection in front of him.

"You're an angel, Jess. Thanks." He downed a third of it in one go, the sharpness on his tongue making his taste buds weep with joy.

Jess smiled at him, and then her eyes veered covertly to Dylan, making Nate suspect — not for the first time — that she had a thing for his colleague. Dylan was either blind, gay, or dumb to not notice it. Maybe all three. He hung out at the bar plenty when she was working. They talked a lot and seemed to be buddies but nothing more. Jess might be a few years younger, but she was pretty, had a superb rack, and was one hell of a bartender.

"I know," she said. "Angel of beer. Heard it before."

She disappeared into the back room, where the food was prepared. Seconds later, Macey Severson, owner of the Shell Shack and wife of Derek, one of the other firefighters, peeked her head around the corner. Nate lifted his chin and smiled in greeting. She came out, wiping her hands on the apron at her waist.

"Hey, Mr. Hero. Heard you had quite the night." Macey came around the end of the bar and hugged him. "Congrats on the rescue."

Nate grinned, deciding to go along with all the to-do. "Dylan's got my dinner, Jess picked up this beautiful cup of hops and barley ... you gonna treat me to a gourmet dessert or what?"

"Or what. How 'bout if I cook your food?" Macey said.

"Guess I'll take it. What are you doing here tonight anyway?" Nate asked. "Thought you were giving most of your time to your nonprofit."

"Just here for the dinner hour," she said. "Mike hurt his back and couldn't make it in, so I'm covering."

"Who's got the princess? Big Daddy?" Dylan asked, referring to their daughter and Macey's husband.

"Derek and Maddy went to a movie. A special showing of some My Little Pony feature." Macey pursed her lips to hide her amusement.

"Excellent," Dylan said. "Derek will be right in his element with the rainbows and stars."

"He's a good daddy," Macey said with a wide grin. She straightened the salt and pepper and napkin holder on the bar and became serious. "He said they suspect arson?"

Nate's empty stomach twisted into a knot. "In the office building fire? I hadn't heard."

"Where you been all day, man?" Dylan asked. "They think it was started right outside of the end unit where you found the woman."

"Outside of Sophie's office? What the fuck?" Nate clenched his fist, and rage boiled up inside him at the thought of some worthless piece of shit intentionally starting a fire.

"Sophie?" Dylan raised one brow as if Nate was one taco short of a combo plate.

"The woman. Sophie Alexander."

"Didn't realize you were on a first-name basis with her. How's she doing?"

"Concussion and smoke inhalation. They'll keep her for a couple days max. Is Grif on the case?" The arsonist bastard needed to be caught. Like, yesterday. Penn Griffin might be one of the newer investigators, but he wasn't new to the fire service, and Nate trusted him implicitly.

"Yep."

"Derek said she was lucky the wind carried the fire away from her office," Macey said. "It could've been a lot worse."

"I think she'd fallen before I found her," Nate said. "That'd explain the head injury. The fire stayed just south of her suite. Had her office been more directly involved … yeah." A spark of cold fear went down his spine. "Bad news. Suspects yet?"

Dylan shook his head, a grim expression on his face.

"Not the last I heard," Macey confirmed. "It's early though."

Until they caught him, there was always the fear that he'd strike again. Nate couldn't help but wonder if Sophie had been the target or it'd been a random hit. And there she was … alone in that hospital bed.

Jess came out of the kitchen with a basket of food and set it in front of him.

"Thanks, Jess. Guess I'm slacking in my duties," Macey said.

"As the owner, you can get away with that," Dylan said. "At least when you have Jess the Angel of Beer on the clock."

Nate ignored the chatter. Ignored them. Just about ignored the food in front of him, but he figured that would get their notice. He shoved a distracted stream of fries in his mouth and rethought his decision on Sophie Alexander.

Looked like he wasn't quite ready to walk away after all.

4

____

Sophie might still feel like her lungs had been used as a punching bag, but she'd never been the type to sit around and do nothing, and she wasn't doing well with the prospect now.

She was going flipping nuts lying in this hospital bed. Going on forty-eight hours so far, and frankly, she was shocked they'd kept her this long. The nausea and headache were mostly gone, and the worst thing was pain in her throat and lungs, but lying here wouldn't make them get better any faster.

She longed to be home in her small beachfront condo. Craved the familiarity and security of it as she never had before, even though she was a homebody through and through. It, too, would be quiet, but at least there she could move. Do something. Really, she wanted to be pretty much anywhere but stuck in this lonely, suffocating hospital room with nothing to do but watch daytime TV or think.

She'd never been much of a TV person, but compared to the thoughts knocking around in her brain, soap operas and talk shows didn't seem so bad today. She'd had the television on for most of the morning, and though she had trouble concentrating on it, due to drifting off to sleep periodically, being hazy from pain meds, and having her mind wander when she was awake, the sound at least filled the room and made it less lonely.

Punching the volume up a couple levels, she tried to get interested in the dramatic woman on the screen's diatribe, but within moments, Sophie's mind was back on what she'd been trying to ignore for hours: she'd come *this* close to dying in a fire.

Dying.

How did someone even process that?

Had the fire department not found her at the exact moment they had, she likely would've lost consciousness in a matter of minutes and then died of asphyxiation. And then … what?

If she'd died, what would've become of Green Systems? Her company that specialized in making old, often historical structures more efficient and environmentally friendly? Her blood, sweat, tears, and livelihood for the past three years? What would have happened to her creation had she burned to ashes in that fire?

Yeah, she knew the answer. *Nothing.*

Green Systems would've gone away. Her name would live on in a couple of trade magazine articles from the recent past, for jobs she'd already done and awards she'd won, but the company itself… *Poof.* No more. And no one would likely miss it.

Her tastefully decorated two-bedroom condo would've been sold, her SUV sold, her personal belongings liquidated or trashed, since there was no one who'd be interested in them. No one who'd find any sentimental value in any aspect of her life.

And her funeral … that would've been a joke. Her assistant, Iona, would've shown up, and her hair girl, Lotti, if her schedule wasn't booked solid with highlights and cuts. There were a few business associates Sophie had formed professional relationships with in the three years since she'd started Green Systems, but most of them were not local, and she doubted many of them cared enough to pay their final respects.

God. Enough of those thoughts. Enough what-ifs.

She had survived. The firefighter had found her in time. And though she'd never asked his name, his concerned eyes and his warm voice had been imprinted onto her brain. She'd have to make a point, after she was released, to track him down and thank him. Somehow.

How in the name of God was it possible to thank a person for saving your life?

She shuddered, and her head pounded harder. She wasn't accustomed to being indebted to anyone, for small things, even, let alone such an enormous one.

Work was a much more comfortable thing to ponder, more routine, and sometimes when things were too vast and mind-blowing to grasp onto, routine was a good place to default to.

At four a.m., when she'd awakened mostly alert for the first time since the fire, she'd started a list of everything she could remember that was likely destroyed in her office. Hello, depression. Now she turned to a new page on the pharmaceutical-ad notepad the nurse had found for her and wrote the heading: To Do. Much less disheartening than To Replace.

It was a fight, but she managed to write down a couple of client names she knew she owed information. Her brain wasn't cooperating because, no matter what she tried, it was kind of caught up on the whole *if she'd died* crap.

"Hey, you." Iona spoke at the same moment she tapped on the open door and poked her head around the corner into Sophie's room.

"Oh, thank God," Sophie said, smiling for real for the first time since the fire as she took in her assistant's familiar, shoulder-length, sand-colored hair and her pink, round cheeks. "Save me from the quiet."

"Thank God is right." Iona set down her bag and rushed to the side of the bed to hug Sophie. "Thank God you're okay. You look good."

"Is lying to me part of your job description?" Sophie asked, her smile fading to a grimace. "Because I look like I got dragged by a freight train."

"You look better than a dead girl. Scared the stuffing out of me when I heard what happened! And then they wouldn't let me in to see you. They'd only connect me to your room phone, which you didn't answer. I should've told them I was your sister from the beginning."

"I was out of it all day yesterday. Didn't even hear the

phone."

The nurse had told her the firefighter had camped out in her room for hours while Sophie had slept, and she'd clung to that knowledge all day. The thought that he'd stayed for so long should make her uncomfortable but instead, it made her feel safe. Like someone out there cared. Two someones — her rescuer and her assistant. Though letting people in wasn't her norm, it felt good to have those two in her corner, especially while she was down.

"I've got a replacement iPhone on its way," Iona said. "I had the business number temporarily forwarded to my cell so we wouldn't miss any calls, and I brought your home laptop, like you asked."

"You're a godsend, Iona. Thank you."

Sophie felt her antsiness seep out of her as she realized how lucky she was. Lucky to have such a capable, reliable woman on her side, among other things.

Maybe it was time to make Iona, who'd earned her environmental engineering degree a year ago while working for Sophie part-time and had been working full-time ever since, a junior partner. Someone who shared in the company's successes and challenges officially. In a tangible way instead of just as glorified support staff. Then if, God forbid, anything ever did happen to Sophie, the thing she'd put so much effort into would live on, at the very least.

Sharing didn't come easy for her, but she could see now why it would be a good idea. She thought, for the first time, maybe she was ready to try sharing.

Sophie took several swallows of water to soothe her still-raw throat. "Pull up a chair."

"Do you know how long you'll be here?" Iona asked as she dragged the chair the firefighter had used close to the bed again and sat down.

"I should go home tomorrow." Sophie raised the head of her bed more so that she was fully upright. "In the meantime, I'm losing my concussed mind in this place."

Iona pulled out two laptops from her bag and set the Mac Air with the floral-patterned skin in pinks and oranges across Sophie's lap.

Iona opened the other computer and powered up. "Before I forget, I talked to Jack. Your test is postponed indefinitely—"

"To get my black belt," Sophie said, wondering how she'd forgotten the event she'd been training for for years. "It was supposed to be Saturday. What day is this?"

"Today is Thursday. You're not testing anytime soon."

As much as Sophie instinctively wanted to argue, there was no denying she wouldn't be ready by the weekend. She'd have to ask the doctor how soon she could return to krav maga. "I'll call Jack later to set a new date."

"He'll be happy to hear from you. He sounded more than a little freaked out." Iona paused while she typed something in. "So, we need to get the bid out to Herman Brandt ASAP. The final, proofed version is in your inbox, waiting for you. I've contacted Mr. Brandt to let him know what happened, and he said not to rush, but if he wants to meet the timeline his museum board set, we need to push it."

Herman Brandt. In Massachusetts. The bid was for greening up a grand, Italianate-style house built in 1843 that now served as a small museum. Sophie reclined her head onto the mattress, feeling at once exhilarated as details of the heating and cooling system overhaul filled her mind and leery of the strong pull to dive right in to the project again. Her work was almost like a drug ... one hit and the nurses down the hall probably saw a change in her vitals. Maybe not such a good thing.

"Thanks. I'll look at it. Soon." She made a silent vow to herself not to do it until she was home — which would be doable only because there was no Wi-Fi at the hospital. She'd always suspected her extreme dedication to her work was borderline unhealthy but had never let herself take time to worry much about it. But was that the person she wanted to be? If she were to die tomorrow — or two nights ago — would she be able to say she'd lived a full life?

"We also need to check in on the Lexington job," Iona said as she undoubtedly read off one of her many super-efficient checklists on her screen. "As well as follow up with Bill MacLevich, email the people from Leeds, talk to—"

"Iona?"

Iona turned her head toward Sophie, her mouth still open. "Yes?"

Sophie handed her the Mac from her lap and shifted onto her side, toward her assistant. She extended her arm, her hand hovering close to Iona's, and hesitated. Then she lowered it and rested her fingers on the back of Iona's wrist. "That stuff can wait."

Iona straightened, looking alarmed. "Of course. God, I'm sorry, Sophie." She hit a few keys, then closed the laptop. "How insensitive am I? I just assumed—"

"You assumed that, since I'm normally *all business*, I would want to get right down to it," Sophie said with a self-conscious smile.

Iona grinned back and squeezed Sophie's hand. "Maybe a little. You're not generally one to waste any time, and when you asked me to bring your laptop—"

"No need to explain. I totally understand."

Sophie studied her assistant's practical-length fingernails, painted in a mellow pink that matched the color in her cheeks. She'd always kept a certain distance between herself and Iona. While they made an amazing, ass-kicking team professionally, she'd made a point of not letting it cross over too far into friendship.

But Sophie suddenly needed a friend. More, she wanted one.

Head injury be damned.

"I trust you to hold down the fort, Iona. I thought I wanted nothing more than to dive in and get back to work, but … I'm tired. And I have you. Right?"

"Absolutely. Whatever you need."

"Right now, it's nice to just have someone here. Do you mind?"

"Of course not. Let me…" Iona slid the two computers back into her bag and rustled through the outer pocket of it. She pulled out a plastic baggie of…

"Trail mix?" Sophie said, sitting up. She went through home-made trail mix like a junkie went through crack cocaine. "Oh, my God, you are the best!"

"Figured the food here sucked." She handed the homemade mixture of nuts, coconut flakes, and raisins to Sophie, who dug in and then shared.

Sophie threw a handful in her mouth just as she remembered how much it hurt to swallow anything harder than a milkshake. "Mmm. The taste is divine." She chewed and chewed, long after she normally would have swallowed. Finally, she forced the food down, and tears sprang up in her eyes. "I think I'm going to have to save it for later. But thank you. So…"

Sophie took a drink to wash down the pain. Then she endeavored to push all things work-related out of her mind, even though those seemed the easiest to talk about. She'd told Iona to put away work for a reason—even if she didn't know much about this friend thing her injured brain seemed to be set on. "I'm so glad you came. Turns out hospitals are crazy quiet."

"Lonely," Iona said. "I remember from when I had my appendix out in college. Even though it's always so noisy when you want to sleep—"

"Exactly! Although I didn't have any problem sleeping yesterday, I guess."

"That's good. You needed it."

"My timing was not good, actually," Sophie said, thinking about the nameless firefighter and trying to get up the nerve to tell Iona about him. She longed to tell her, but … this *sharing* concept. It didn't come naturally to her.

"Oh? What'd you miss?"

"Well, you know I was carried out of the burning building by a firefighter, right?"

Iona nodded and leaned closer, her eyes widening expectantly.

Sophie took a steadying breath, closed her eyes for a moment, and saw … him. "Turns out he's … oh, my God, he's so good-looking. And he hung out in my room yesterday. All day. While I slept…"

5

W ithout opening her eyes, Sophie groaned, wishing the nurse who was grabbing at her hand would give it a rest. She was hospital-ed out. Vital-ed out. Everything-ed out.

"No more," she mumbled, trying to sink back into sleep. God, she was so tired.

"Hey."

The voice was a man's, and his hand was still on hers. Her eyes popped open.

Her firefighter was here again.

Her defenses melted, and she turned her head toward him, grasping his hand, letting her eyes droop shut again. Time passed, and she might have drifted off … maybe for a minute. Maybe for five. When the bed dipped lower on his side by her waist, her brain fired up, and she opened her eyes. He sat on the thin mattress, his butt warm and solid up against her middle in order to fit.

She gripped his fingers more tightly and tried to smile.

"Hi, Sophie. Okay if I move this?" He gestured to the rolling table with her cold dinner on it.

She nodded sleepily. "What time is it?"

"Little after eight p.m."

Iona had sat with her for the whole afternoon and they'd

done something Sophie hadn't done for eons — watched a movie. A chick flick, no less, just like girlfriends would. And it'd been pretty flipping awesome once she'd relaxed and, well, gotten over herself. Her assistant — *friend* — had taken off when they'd brought Sophie's tray full of carbs plus a tiny slab of dry turkey, also known as dinner. Sophie must have crashed not long after picking at the turkey and then pushing the tray away. Her stomach growled now.

The firefighter laughed quietly, and Sophie frowned, embarrassed. "The food here..." She made a face.

"Sucks?"

"I'm sure it's fine if you don't mind white grains. Bread. Noodles. Cookies."

"You don't eat cookies?"

"Not often."

"Explains why you're so light. You should eat cookies."

He'd carried her, she remembered. "You know my approximate body weight. I should know your name."

He laughed again, a low rumble that warmed her. "That and you should know the names of guys who sit on your hospital bed. Nate Rottinghaus."

"Nate," she repeated. She nodded, trying to find the right words for what she needed to say, even though she and Iona had discussed it at length. Owing someone her life was unfamiliar territory.

She attempted to clear her throat, but that hurt. Rough, unsexy voice it was, then. "Nate," she said again. "Thank you for saving my life." Her sore throat swelled up around the words and her eyes dampened. She swallowed hard in order to continue, but nothing else came to her. "Just ... thanks."

"I was just doing my job." His tone was light, as if to brush off her thanks.

"Maybe, but..." She shook her head, afraid if she said more her voice would crack or one of those damn tears would actually run down her face and embarrass her.

Nate squeezed her hand and encased it between both of his. She soaked up the reassurance, the security of his strong, tanned hands protecting her smaller one. Tried to remember the last time she'd held a man's hand and felt like this. Scratch that — she hadn't felt like this. She'd held a few hands, been with a few guys, but she'd usually been too preoccupied or too worried about their next move to appreciate much.

"You seem to be doing better," Nate said, saving her again, this time by changing the subject when she was so worked up. She wasn't sure how she felt about this rescue habit of his.

"How's your head feel?" he asked.

Sophie frowned. "How did you know I hit my head?"

"Nurse mentioned it when I was here yesterday."

"Was that only yesterday? It seems like a week."

"I would've come sooner today but I worked half a shift for a buddy. Just got done at seven."

"You didn't have to come," Sophie said, feeling suddenly panicky because of his intent and the way it made her heart do a little dip. "You've gone over and above the call of duty. Way beyond."

"Maybe this has nothing to do with duty." He rubbed his thumb back and forth over her hand, his touch gentle. Soothing.

Too soothing.

She pulled her hand away, running it through her hair, trying to play it off. Which reminded her, her hair was bad news. She'd managed a shower earlier, but she'd been too worn out to blow-dry her hair or do anything to it.

"Your hair looks fine," Nate said as if he'd known her for years and could read her every thought.

Sophie swallowed nervously. Summoned the energy to shift herself upward and over, putting a couple of inches between them. She fiddled with the bed controls, raising the head a few degrees.

Nate stood abruptly. Looked instantly uncomfortable, as if maybe he hadn't planned on getting so cozy either. His eyes flicked to the floor, allowing a flash of insecurity to show before he shoved it aside. But she'd seen it. And it eased her mind a little. Allowed her to relax her shoulders.

He was an honorable guy — she knew it instinctively. He

apparently felt compelled to make sure she was okay. There was no reason for the tension in her gut.

Lie.

He was too good-looking, with his quiet concern in those beautiful hazel eyes and his stubbled, square jaw that, if she was honest, made her want to reach out and run her fingers over it. And the arms, oh, my God, the arms. He wore a plain hunter-green T-shirt, and his biceps bulged out of the sleeves for all the world to admire. No wonder he'd said she was light — he could probably lift four times her weight with those muscles. He turned toward her, and she took in the broadness of his shoulders, the narrowness of his hips. She forced her eyes to meet his.

"You never answered my question," he said.

Her brain felt scrambled, and it wasn't from her head injury. Her mouth was suddenly dry, so dry, and she couldn't for the life of her remember what he'd asked. "What...?"

"Your head? Better?"

"Oh." She nodded. "Everything's good enough that I get to go home tomorrow."

"That's great. What time?"

"As soon as the doctor releases me. After his morning rounds, the nurse said."

"I'll give you a ride."

"You don't need to do that." It was one thing to be with him here, in the hospital room. Here, she was the fire victim he'd saved, the patient he was checking on. Outside these walls, she didn't know what they were, but the way he made her insides warm and melty ... that was scary.

He glanced around the room. "You don't... Where's your family, Sophie?"

"I don't have any."

Nate frowned. "None?"

"My mom died a week after I turned eighteen. I've been on my own ever since." All true. Her dad hadn't even been there for her years ago when he'd lived with them. And her brother... Who knew where he was these days? She hadn't laid eyes on him for years.

"I'm sorry—"

"It's okay. It's been a long time."

"It's just my dad and me," Nate said, pulling the chair close to her bed and sitting. "He's a fire lieutenant, so we're tight."

"You work together?" She gladly latched onto the topic of his family to get away from hers.

"Yep. We worked together all day."

"Have you heard if they figured out the cause of the fire?" She'd been curious, couldn't help wondering during the endless hours by herself before Iona had come. She'd questioned Iona, as well, but if anyone knew the cause, it hadn't hit the media yet. The more she wondered, the more she needed to know.

Nate pressed his lips together, a minute movement, before he spoke. "There's always talk." He didn't meet her gaze, and she wouldn't have thought anything of it if she hadn't noticed his unwavering eye contact up until now.

"You know, don't you?" she said.

"It's early. No conclusive evidence the last I heard."

She narrowed her eyes, studying him. He was speaking too carefully. And he hadn't given her a flat-out no. Which she suspected meant yes. "It's bad, isn't it?"

His Adam's apple bobbed as he swallowed. "A few more minutes and you wouldn't have made it out of that fire alive, Sophie. I'd say that's bad." His voice was thick with emotion, and that got to her. A knot pulsed in her throat, threatening to prevent her lungs from getting enough air.

Because of him, she was here. Alive.

She fought the deluge of emotion — gratitude, fear, even some anger that either of them had been put in that position. She massaged her temples and forced air into her windpipe, past the lump in her throat. Refocused her mind on the facts, which were always safer than feelings.

"Was it Mrs. Forester?"

"Was what Mrs. Forester?" Finally, Nate looked at her.

"The fire. Did she leave a candle burning or something?" At his blank look, she explained, "The old woman in the office suite next to mine. She proclaims to be a psychic. She brings her cat, Nefertiti, to the office on a leash. I … worry about her."

"Worry how?"

"I don't think she's all there. She used to forget which door was hers until she put the foil door cover of the sparkly, gold angel up."

The room phone rang, startling both of them. Nate motioned to the nightstand against the wall, back behind and to her left, and she nodded, knowing it was Iona and that Iona would get a kick out of "her firefighter" answering her phone after the way Sophie had rattled on about him earlier.

"Sophie's room." He stood next to her shoulders and listened. "Just a moment, sir."

Sophie was trying to figure out what "sir" would be calling her when Nate held out the phone with a puzzled look.

"William Alexander would like to speak to his daughter," he said. "I assume that's you."

Her blood went cold at the name. "Technically speaking." She stared at the receiver, searching her mind for a way to avoid talking to the man. Finding none, she took it as her stomach tightened into a rock.

"Yes?"

"Sophie, sweetheart, I just heard what happened. I wanted to make sure you're okay."

Sweetheart? Were they putting hallucinogens in her IV? "I'm fine." Or she had been until she'd heard the sound of his voice.

"It sounds like you've been through an ordeal. Is there anything I can do? Do you need anything?"

Stunned, she took a while to form a response. She'd needed something years and years ago. Something like … a father.

"I'm… No. I don't need anything from you."

Why was he calling her? Acting like he cared? He'd proven he didn't time and again. What was more, she'd finally accepted it, for the most part. Ages ago. The only question was why she was still on the phone with him.

"Please don't call me again," she said, her voice hard, as cold as she could make it. She held the receiver out to Nate to hang up as a wave of nausea overcame her.

Nate hung up and then, instead of returning to his chair as she wanted him to, he stood close. Sophie worked to force down her reaction. Of all the times her dad could crash back into her life, he had to choose now, when Nate was here.

I just learned your name — here's my dirty laundry.

He put his hand on her shoulder and squeezed gently, without a word. She braced herself for his questions, because how could you witness *that* phone call, after she'd said she had no family, and not ask questions?

"I haven't talked to him for over two years, when he called to congratulate me on an industry award I won. Before that, it was over ten years," she said, letting her hair fall like a privacy curtain over the side of her face. "I definitely don't consider him family if you're wondering why I said I have none."

"I understand." Nate pulled the chair near her shoulders, sat on it, and ran his fingers over her hand, back and forth, conveying without words that he was on her side. She couldn't remember the last time she'd had someone on her side. She liked it, and yet it made her uncomfortable.

"So anyway," she said, shifting to sit up straighter, mostly as an excuse to pull her hand away from his. "You were telling me what you know about the fire."

He stared at her for a moment, maybe debating whether he'd let her get away with the subject change.

"Mrs. Forester?" she reminded him.

His expression changed, and she could tell he'd flipped back into business mode. "I don't think it was Mrs. Forester," Nate said, fidgeting. He lowered his voice and leaned closer, elbows on his thighs, hands rubbing over his stubbled jaw. "Look, Sophie, if I tell you more, you have to swear not to breathe a word of it. Not to anyone. I could get in trouble at work."

"Of course. Who would I tell anyway?" She gestured to the empty room.

"Even once you're out of here. Not a word."

A thread of cold fear crept through her gut. Sophie nodded.

Nate stood again and walked to the door. He shut it quietly and came back to the side of the bed. This time, he sat on the mattress instead of the chair.

"As I said, they're waiting for tests to come back as conclusive evidence," he said, keeping his voice so quiet she had to strain to hear, "but they suspect the fire was arson."

The thread of fear expanded to fill her like a block of concrete. "Someone … did that on purpose?"

"It appears that way." There was a hard edge to his voice, and his jaw was set. "Son of a bitch deserves to burn alive."

She closed her eyes, trying to absorb the news. "They just destroyed … so much…" Her office, her computer, most of her paper records, her sketches and blueprints for all of the current projects… Yes, she did a lot of her work online, and she could access most of that from the laptop she'd kept at home, but there were drawers full of her three-year-old company in that one office suite, and it was all gone.

She bit down on the inside of her mouth until it bled. "I'll be the one to light the bastard on fire. Are there suspects?" A firing squad would also work, but only if she got to fire the gun.

"Not to my knowledge. Shit, Sophie, maybe I shouldn't have told you—"

"No, it's fine. I needed to know."

"It's a lot to absorb. Do you have friends you could call for moral support once it becomes public knowledge?"

She thought of Iona. Yeah, things had changed for the better today, but Sophie couldn't see whining about this to her. "I'll be okay, Nate. Thank you for telling me."

"When the investigator gets the test results back, he and probably the fire chief will come in to tell you. You can't let on that you already know."

"I won't."

He stared at her, his eyes narrowed with doubt.

"I won't, Nate. I don't want you to get in trouble."

"It'll become a criminal investigation—"

"I understand." She sat up straighter and touched his arm, an uncharacteristic gesture for her, but she wanted to reassure him since he'd put himself on the line for her.

More than once.

He twisted his arm and took her hand in his, the cords of muscle in his forearm shifting impressively beneath her fingers.

"I told you because I want you to be careful, especially once you leave here tomorrow."

Sophie frowned and took in the contrast of their hands — his long, capable fingers dwarfing her whole petite hand. Normally, she felt so competent, able to handle whatever she needed to by herself, but a wave of weakness rolled over her.

Why would someone set her building on fire? Had they targeted her specifically? There were seven other suites, all of them but one occupied, so anyone could've been the target. Had it been random? The questions were too frightening to utter out loud.

She nodded. "I'll be careful. I always am."

"I'm picking you up tomorrow."

"There's no need—"

"I'm going to make sure you get home safely." His jaw was set stubbornly, and his eyes penetrated hers, warning that he wouldn't take no for an answer.

And while part of her reveled in the way he seemed determined to continue this … *whatever* was going on between them, another, bigger part of her was more than a little scared.

6

Nate didn't get out and about before nine a.m. on his days off for just anyone.

Shit. He'd known Sophie for three days, and already, she wasn't just anyone. He was drawn to her, physically, sure, but there was more to it. She'd looked banged up and exhausted for as long as he'd known her, and yet he couldn't stay away. There was no explanation, and he refused to think too hard about it as he parked in the visitor lot of the hospital and headed for the door. He had to make himself move at a normal pace instead of rushing inside to see her.

Good damn thing he slowed down too. Otherwise he might've missed the nurse rolling Sophie's wheelchair out to a waiting cab on the other side of the entrance. He jogged over to her and fell into step with the nurse.

"I can get her from here," he said, working to keep his frustration out of his voice.

Sophie's head whipped around toward him. "Nate." She managed to sound surprised.

"That taxi is waiting for her," the nurse said, nodding toward the first car in a line of them waiting to pick up passengers.

"I'll take care of him," Nate said, forcing his I'm-a-firefighter-everything-will-be-okay smile. "And her."

36

"You comfortable with this, Sophie?" The nurse leaned to Sophie's side to reassure herself.

"Yeah, I... He... Yes. This is the man who rescued me, Elizabeth. He apparently thinks his work isn't done yet and he has to get me home safely." Sophie's lips curved up into a tantalizing shy grin.

At the sight of that smile, his tension started to melt away.

"Oooh." The nurse straightened and looked at him again, this time with less glare and more *hel-lo*, the tone of feminine appreciation he used to get a kick out of when he was a rookie. "I guess there are tougher burdens to bear, my dear. I need to take my trusty chair with me though. You okay to stand?"

Sophie answered by clutching the plastic hospital-logo bag in her lap and rising to her feet. Her skin still seemed pale to Nate, but he'd never seen her when she was healthy, so maybe that was her usual coloring. Or maybe she was just still recuperating from some scum of the earth nearly killing her. Either way, he was one hundred percent entranced by her.

The nurse reached out for Sophie's hand. "You take care, okay, sweetie? If you have any questions on your self-care, you call that number on the paper."

"I will. Thanks for everything. You're the best."

The nurse wheeled the empty chair away from them and went back inside. Nate told the cabbie Sophie had a ride, and then he glanced across the lot.

"My truck is parked about halfway down that first row. If I go get it, will you still be here when I drive up?"

Sophie closed her eyes momentarily against the light-headedness from standing. She'd done almost nothing but lie around for two days and was weak as a kitten ... and detested that feeling.

As she waited for the dizziness to level out, she felt Nate's hand, firm but gentle, on her arm, steadying her. She opened her eyes to find him inches away, frowning with concern.

"I'm okay. Just rusty at this standing thing. I can make it to your truck as long as we don't sprint."

"I'll drive up."

"It's not that far. I can walk."

"I could carry you." He grinned and raised his brows, letting on he wasn't serious, and that alone saved him.

"I have a head injury and charbroiled lungs, not a broken leg. I want to walk." She swallowed and stiffened her spine, feeling steadier now, and more determined. The sooner she could start walking, standing, doing anything besides lying in a hospital room, the sooner she'd get her strength back.

Nate looked about to say no, so Sophie tried a different tack. She wrapped her hand around his upper arm and held on. "Please?"

He took her bag from her and nodded. "Let's go then."

When they got to his truck, an older but well taken care of Ford, she let him help her up into it and sank into the seat, way more tired than she should be from walking a few hundred feet. Recuperation was going to get on her nerves.

Nate climbed in on his side, shot a quick, assessing glance her way, then started the truck. The radio blared out a country song, and he hit the power button to silence it. "Where do you live?"

"Sea Breeze Condominiums on the island. Do you know them?"

"They're at Sea Breeze Drive, right?"

She nodded, and he headed toward the bridge that would take them across the bay to San Amaro.

"Don't think you're off the hook for trying to ditch me this morning," he said lightly as they drove over the shallow bay.

Damn. Busted. She'd been hoping they could just gloss over that. "I'm sorry. They released me, and you weren't there, so—"

"So you left me hanging. Or would have."

"I didn't know if you'd show up," she said quietly, voicing only one of her numerous concerns. Another was that he *would* show up. And here she was, torn between being annoyed and grateful. And more.

It was the *more* that scared the shit out of her.

"I said I'd drive you home. Of course I'd show up."

"I get that now," she said sheepishly. "I apologized. What else do you want from me?"

"Dinner."

That.

That was exactly why this was a bad idea.

"I'm supposed to be recovering, not going out."

"Who said anything about 'out'? I'll leave you alone to sleep all day, and then I'll come back at dinnertime to cook you something. That will save you from having to cook. See? All about recovery."

"You're hard to argue with."

"Resistance is futile."

Sophie laughed in spite of her reluctance. Then she sobered, the butterflies in her gut intensifying. "Why are you doing this?"

"Doing what?"

"Everything. Visiting me in the hospital, putting yourself on the line to tell me what you weren't supposed to tell me — which, by the way, the fire chief and the investigator did visit me this morning and confirmed that it was arson — taking me home, cooking me dinner—"

"So dinner's a yes then." He shot a shit-eating grin her way, and even when he was being smug, her heartbeat still did a little double-time beat just from how good-looking he was.

"Just dinner," she said. "It's not a date."

"Not a date." Nate nodded.

Those were the words she needed to hear, and yet they brought her no comfort.

7

It was a lucky thing this wasn't a date, Sophie thought hazily as she sprang out of bed from a sound sleep. Her head spun, so she leaned against the wall momentarily, eyes closed.

The knocking came again, and she was pretty sure the doorbell had rung a couple of times before her brain had engaged and she'd realized it must be Nate, the unrelenting hero.

"Be right there," she hollered, keeping a hand on the hallway wall as she made her way to the main entry, wondering how long her concussion would keep her off-balance.

She looked through the peephole, then opened the door, focusing only on getting there before he gave up on her — not on how she looked. That god-awful truth hit her as soon as she and Nate stood face-to-face and his gaze darted from hers down to her bare toes and back up, over her baggy, unflattering, old sleep shirt and boxers.

"Hello, sleepyhead," he said.

Sophie groaned and rubbed a hand over her face before stepping back to let him in. It was all she could do not to dart back out of sight to her room to hide — not just because of her appearance but because the look on his face, the smile ... it was too intimate.

She straightened instead, doing a mental inventory of where

her shirt ended (just below the hem of her boxers) and how see-through it was (enough — way more than enough). Crossing her arms over her chest, she shivered. "I'm going to get dressed. Help yourself to the kitchen," she added as the large paper grocery bag in his arms registered. "I'll be five minutes."

"Take your time. Relax."

Easier said than done, thanks to the sparkle of interest in his eyes and the way his gaze kept sinking to her too-thin shirt and her bare legs. She attempted an unbothered smile. Likely failed.

"I've got dinner," he said. "You're not allowed to help."

"I meant to wake up hours ago." She said it to his back as he went into the kitchen and set the bag on the counter.

"You needed to sleep, Sophie. Operation Recovery." He busied himself unloading the bag, and the unassuming smile he aimed her way sent that same warm sensation he'd given her in the hospital deep into her chest. It wasn't rational. He was still almost a stranger. But she clung to it anyway and admitted to herself she was a little bit glad he was here.

When she reemerged, dressed in leggings and an oversized zip-up hoodie, hair combed, mortification from the way it'd looked when she'd opened the door mostly gone, she found Nate outside on her sixth-floor balcony.

The sliding glass door was closed, giving her a moment to take in the delicious sight of him from the back, leaning against the railing, looking out at the gulf. There was enough separation between them, or maybe her guard was just down enough, that she saw him more objectively, instead of as a threat to her equilibrium. Just a beautiful, strong, sexy man with a killer ass. Like an action-movie lead, all virile and dripping with testosterone.

In her condo.

If she were more adventurous — okay, more trusting and open — she'd probably lure him down the hall to her bed and have the night of her life. But that wasn't the way she was or had ever been.

It occurred to her maybe she'd been living her life the wrong way.

Shaking her head against that uneasy thought, she snapped

into action and opened the door. When she stepped outside, the wind gusted through her hair. It was chilly but refreshing. *Fresh. Alive.* The complete opposite of the sterile, still hospital air.

Sophie walked past the two mint-condition teak lounge chairs with their fluffy, never-used cushions to sidle up to the railing right next to Nate. Her eyes were drawn to the drama of the waves crashing wildly on this windy, cloudy day. Everything was varying shades of gray — the sky, the waves, the beach — and yet it was full of life and action and possibility somehow. Something inside of her sparked to life.

Nate draped his arm across her back, his hand settling on her opposite hip and pulling her into his side. And she let him. Relished the comfort, the heat of his body.

"Great balcony," he said. "Do you use it much?"

"I don't really have time to. In fact, in the eighteen months I've lived here, I never have." She frowned. "It's beautiful, isn't it? Even on a not-so-beautiful day."

Sophie breathed in deeply — without coughing, even — probably more deeply than she had in a week, or maybe a year, and closed her eyes. Allowed the briney, damp sea air to infiltrate her still-healing lungs, her senses. She felt it on her skin, smelled it, tasted it like she hadn't in ages. Her head swam with a troubling realization as she opened her eyes again to the overwhelming, magnificent view. "I could've died without ever appreciating this." She flung her arms out to both sides. "That's sad."

"But now you can," Nate said in a gentle voice that soothed her.

"I've been kind of tunnel-visioned. Blind to everything but work, but if I'd died, none of that would matter." She swallowed hard. Sure, she'd changed some buildings for the better here and there, and she liked to think what she did was important but if she didn't do it, someone else would. Eventually. That hard truth seeped in and shook her to the core.

"We're all just doing the best we can, Soph. You believe in what you do. That's something not everyone can say."

"You believe in what you do too," she said, looking up at him, feeling a jolt to her core when his eyes met hers.

"I do. If I didn't, chances are we wouldn't be standing here right now."

"*I* wouldn't be standing here right now." She barely noticed her eyes had watered up as she turned back to watch the layers of waves roll in. Other than her pursuit of a black belt in krav maga, which she also treated more like a job than a hobby, her entire life was Green Systems. That wasn't really a life, was it? It was missing out on … other stuff. Everything else.

It was possible to work one's butt off and still have more. Wasn't it? "What do you do when you're not working?" she asked him.

"Me? All kinds of stuff. Play volleyball, basketball, softball, watch sports, go out with the guys, fish a little bit. I try to get hockey tickets a few times a season." He shrugged. "Whatever comes up, I guess."

"I can't remember the last time I did 'whatever comes up.'"

"You work all the time?" The fingers of his left hand made little circles at her waist, and his right arm stretched along the railing in front of his body, his hand resting near her, drawing her attention. Coarse hairs dotted the back of it, his fingers relaxed, belying their strength, but she knew firsthand both the power those hands held and the gentleness they were capable of. She had no trouble imagining what they could do to a woman's body, and that's when she dragged her gaze back to his face and jogged her brain to remember his question.

"Yes. I work, I eat, I go to my krav maga workouts, I work some more … sleep…"

"You need an intervention," he said, his tone light, without judgment.

Something about the moment and the man and … who knew what else, probably her brush with death … she was able to see the truth in that. His eyes didn't waver from hers, and she was drawn into their depths, the openness in them, the sparkle of life that came from doing more than just working all the time.

At this moment, she wanted more too.

The sound of the surf roared through her as she turned ninety degrees to face him. He followed suit, his hand slipping to her other hip.

She didn't know how to change the way she was, but she recognized, in this second, she could change this moment. For now, she could take more. Give more.

Live better.

Not stopping to think about what she was doing, Sophie slowly lifted her shaking hand to his chest. Her fingers were met by solid, defined muscle, and she ran both her hands up and down, over the glorious ridges and valleys of his pecs, his upper abs, his shoulders. The pupils of his eyes enlarged, and his hand eased beneath her sweatshirt hem, onto the bare skin of her waist, branding her flesh with his heat.

Her gaze dropped to his lips, to the faint sheen of moisture on them, the need to taste them pulsing through her with every accelerated beat of her heart. She trailed her hands up to the back of his neck and rose to her toes. He leaned down to meet her halfway, and their lips touched. Unsteady breaths mingled. Mouths locked together. Her tongue darted out to explore the soft heat of his lips, to taste him, and it tangled with his, a tentative courtship at first, rapidly becoming a duel of exploration. His facial hair scraped against her skin. Their bodies crushed together and mouths fused, tongues twisting and caressing. Her insides turned to molten liquid as a low, sexy groan escaped from deep in his throat.

The incessant roar of the gulf faded to nothing as her entire existence narrowed to Nate's kiss. His hand burrowed in her hair, holding her close, and his tongue was thorough and seeking and still somehow careful with her.

"Interventions are good," she said, her way of trying to tell him she was fine, that he didn't need to treat her with kid gloves just because she'd just gotten out of the hospital.

She felt his lips smile and his growl vibrate against her suddenly sensitive breasts. As his lips devoured hers, she dropped one hand to his waist and found the hem of his T-shirt, pressed her fingers beyond it to his bare skin. To his flawless, hard abdomen and higher, again to his beautiful sculpted chest.

As her hand kept caressing, exploring, her fingertips brushed over his nipple. A sensitive nipple, judging by the way he moaned again and forgot to be so careful with her.

His reaction was heady, empowering, and the next thing she realized was his hand beneath her sweatshirt, easing its way toward the bottom curve of her breast, dipping beneath her bra. When his work-roughened fingers rasped over her nipple, a shock of sensation shot to her core. Her head swam, and her knees weakened. She grasped on to his sides to keep from swaying from the onslaught.

Nate lightened the kiss and moved his hands to her waist to steady her. "Sophie." His voice was coarse and sexy and *she'd done that to him*. The knowledge was dizzying. "You just got home," he said with some effort. "We need to take it easy."

Her body screamed that she wanted anything but easy, but her confidence wasn't quite there yet and kept her from telling him as she tried to breathe evenly. Forget evenly … just tried to breathe.

"I'm…" Her voice was barely there, so she cleared her throat. "I'm good."

A low, sexy laugh rumbled from his chest. "You are definitely good." He brushed his lips over her jaw, up close to her ear, making her shiver. "But you're still recovering, and I'm being a selfish jackass."

She opened her mouth to argue, and he planted a kiss there. He wove their fingers together, his strong ones dwarfing hers.

"We *will* pick up where we left off. Soon. But I don't want to push you. And I promised you dinner."

As he pierced her with the sincerity in his eyes, she couldn't resist the urge to run her fingers over his scruffy jawline. The soft bristles sprang back and tickled her. Loving the masculine texture, she pressed a kiss to the corner of his mouth, letting the hair abrade her tender lips again.

In spite of the way her body still hummed with the need for more of him, his concern, his consideration evoked an even stronger reaction in her — one that made something catch in her chest. That response was more alarming than the physical one.

She could do sex. There'd been guys in the past who'd had no problem getting her revved up and into bed. But the *something else*, the feelings that didn't fall into the strip-me-naked-now category ... those were more foreign. Something she tended to avoid at the earliest hint. And somehow, this man had sneaked past her early-alert system.

Yes, putting on the brakes was an excellent plan.

As if on cue, her stomach, which she'd neglected all day, rumbled.

Nate laughed, his eyes sparkling, and she wondered if her eyes ever sparkled like that. She had her doubts.

"Apparently, dinner is a fantastic idea."

SEVERAL HOURS LATER, Nate climbed into his truck, adjusting his jeans, which had become too tight in the fly and damn uncomfortable.

The night had been torture. Beautiful, glorious torture. He hadn't fucked up the shrimp scampi he'd cooked for dinner — Sophie either really had loved it or was one hell of an actress. They'd sat side by side at the bar, and as whipped as it made him sound, they'd talked and he'd loved every second of it. He'd never felt like this before, never wanted to soak up everything he could learn about a woman, never been content to listen to one talk about whatever she wanted to talk about.

Fuck. He was in deep.

They'd talked about work (his and hers), the best bars and restaurants on the island (Shell Shack and Raul's), and national economics. She was smart, way too smart for him, but that was a turn-on. Though they hadn't talked about anything too personal, he felt like he knew her well, even though, technically, they'd only known each other for three days — two if you didn't count the day she'd been practically unconscious.

And yet he wanted to know more. Wanted to know everything about her.

And physically ... yeah. When they'd sat on the couch

together watching the Food Network, which she admitted she'd never watched before, and she'd rested her head on his shoulder, he'd paid more attention to the light floral scent of her hair and the way her chest rose and fell with every breath than the TV. Her tits were average size, nothing that would catch a guy's eye, but he wanted nothing more than to feast on them — and the rest of her.

But not tonight. He'd been a fucking saint tonight — except for the scorching good-night kiss she'd initiated and he sure as hell hadn't fought — holding himself back, letting her relax and recover, because if he'd given in to what he really wanted to do, she would've ended up hating him almost as much as he'd hate himself.

He didn't know what he was getting himself into, but if he was honest, he didn't want out. He wanted more. Wanted as much as she would give him. But tonight, while she recuperated from injuries, he'd have to settle for a cold shower.

8

Sophie woke up the next morning wondering if feeling *this* uncomfortable in her own skin could be a result of a head injury.

She threw the covers back and hopped out of bed, a slow-motion kind of hop because she was leery of the light-headedness that'd plagued her for the past couple of days.

Her heart pounded for no reason, and again, she tried to blame her injuries. Tried to. Deep down, she knew the true cause.

Nate.

No, that wasn't even it.

It was herself.

She'd practically thrown herself at him on the balcony last night, and then again before he'd left. What was more, she'd let down her guard the entire evening.

For the first time in her life, the guy had been the one to slow things down instead of her. Had Nate not pulled away, she wasn't sure if she would've stopped short of taking him to her bedroom.

Her body responded even now as she thought about him, but of course, it was primed from a night of hot dreams starring none other than her rescuer. Naked. Inside of her.

Her laptop sat on her dresser, and the urge to open it and start working was so strong she went to it and ran her hand over it, as if the case alone could bring her comfort. But she'd made a promise to herself — and Iona — that she'd wait until Monday morning to jump back in.

It shouldn't be this hard to *not* work.

As she climbed into the shower without letting the water heat up, she gritted her teeth against the cold and started questioning her sanity. She'd read about people who'd developed totally different personalities after a head injury and wondered if that was the case for her.

By the time the water was hot enough, she was rinsing shampoo out of her hair, racing through her routine just to get away from…

What?

As she stepped out onto the extra-thick bath mat and grabbed a towel, she swayed like a drunk. She grabbed her towel and sat down on the closed toilet to try to get control — physically and mentally.

Nate Rottinghaus had her turned inside out like no other man ever had, and she couldn't even say why.

He was good-looking. Okay, more than. His body was cut like a Navy SEAL's, and his beautiful eyes touched something deep inside of her whenever she looked at him. He was hotter than the other guys she'd been with, sure, but it went deeper than that. He was attentive and gentle and comforting and comfortable, and when she was with him, she dropped her guard without even realizing it.

That man had the power to hurt her like she couldn't even imagine.

Sweat beaded on her forehead, and, wrapped in a bath sheet, she darted out of the steamy bathroom as if it were on fire. She whipped open the door to the balcony, hoping the cool air blowing through the living room would cool her down.

Not being a fan of public exposure, she was about to step back from the doorway when the sea air penetrated her brain via her nose. She paused, holding on to the jamb, and breathed it in, letting it flow through her lungs and outward into every cell in her body. After the third breath, the shaking inside of her dissipated, as if sea water had washed over her and taken the shakes with it.

She was drawn outside and stopped short when she felt the cold surface of the balcony under her feet. Glancing in both directions, she assessed the privacy—concrete walls stretched up on both sides, blocking her space from the neighbors'. The railing was thick, transparent plexiglass, but she was six floors up.

Screw it. If someone wanted to ogle her in her towel, they could have a free show. She'd been missing out for too long.

Sophie tightened the towel at her chest and stepped to the railing. The water was bluer today. More vivid. The November wind still whipped, but the sun reflected on the water, so bright she couldn't look directly at it.

The courage the fresh air had inspired in her yesterday returned. The determination to do more than bury herself in her career pulsed in her. When she finally shivered from the cool air, she dragged herself away from the edge of the balcony, went inside, and grabbed her cell phone.

"To girl time," Iona said, holding her champagne flute out to Sophie, who clinked glasses.

"To girl time. This isn't what I expected when I called you." She smiled and took a sip of the light, slightly sweet bubbly, working to let go of the idea that she should be getting a little work done today.

"It's a sin against nature that you've never had a pedicure before," Iona said.

"I didn't know it included champagne or I might have."

"All about priorities — and knowing which spa to hit."

"Feet haven't been at the top of my list, I guess." Sophie leaned back into the massage chair, the champagne warming her insides as her feet soaked. She may have decided her priority list had been flawed, but that didn't mean refocusing was easy.

Iona had been in her car when Sophie had called, and she'd told Sophie to get dressed because she was stopping by in five minutes. After throwing her hair up and pulling on jeans, a sweater, and boots, she'd met Iona out front, deciding once she sat in the front seat of Iona's Camry it was probably best she hadn't had time to think.

Spontaneity wasn't her strong point. Who had time for spontaneity when you worked or thought about work all your waking hours? Though she and Iona shared a strong work ethic, Sophie was realizing they had a lot of differences outside the office. She could stand for some of Iona's habits to rub off on her.

"Your feet will thank you. Trust me," Iona said.

Two spa employees came over to their chairs and went to work pampering them. Sophie felt weird about having anyone touch her feet, but within about two minutes, she was over it and succumbed completely.

"Okay, you could be right," she told Iona, sipping more champagne.

Iona reclined against the luxurious cushion and let out a sigh of bliss as her nail tech began massaging her arches. "How are you feeling, Soph? You look pretty good considering the time I gave you to get ready."

"Yeah, thanks for that."

"Betsy's a busy lady." Iona waved a manicured hand at her tech. "Nobody keeps her waiting."

"Ha," Betsy said. "If only…"

"Is your head feeling better?" Iona asked quietly.

"Mostly. Just a little dizziness every once in a while. I'm feeling good. I…" She looked at the two techs, wondering how much they were listening to their conversation. "Nate cooked me dinner."

Iona leaned forward, and her dark blond brows rose. "Ooh? Firefighter Nate?"

Sophie felt her cheeks heat as her tech, Suri, looked up from the pumice stone she was using on Sophie's feet.

"Sophie was in a fire a few days ago," Iona explained to the two women. "The office building on Garcia that burned?"

"I heard about that on the news," Betsy said. "You were *in* it?"

"Firefighter Nate, who is allegedly one sexy specimen, had to carry her out," Iona said.

"Oh, my God!" Suri gently squeezed Sophie's feet. "You poor thing."

"Poor thing?" Betsy said. "Carried out by a hot firefighter? Sign me up."

"A hot firefighter who cooked her dinner last night," Iona added, and Sophie reminded herself this was allegedly how girl time went. Not that she had any experience with it. Serving alcohol was an effective icebreaker.

"Bet dinner's not all that was cooking," Betsy said, and Sophie couldn't help thinking about the kisses on the balcony, in spite of her reluctance to share with these women she didn't know.

"He was … perfect," Sophie said, finishing up her champagne. "A perfect gentleman." All three women stared at her, waiting for more, and she grinned, feeling the beginning effects of the alcohol. "Even when I didn't want him to be."

Betsy howled, and Iona reached out for Sophie's hand. "You so deserve a good man, Soph. Are you going to see him again?"

"I don't know. I kind of left it in his court."

Both of the nail girls glanced up at her, and Iona let out a quiet "oh." She watched Sophie with a question in her eyes.

"What was I supposed to do?" Sophie asked, knowing full well she was out of her element by a couple hundred zip codes. She couldn't bring herself to admit that Nate had been the one to come to his senses and slow things down. She'd *thought* he'd been into it, would've sworn to it at the time, but now her confidence faltered, and she wasn't sure of anything.

Suri had finished pumicing her feet and walked behind a marble-looking wall for a moment. She returned with the champagne bottle. "You get seconds since it's your first time."

"Heck, give her thirds for being pulled out of a burning building," Betsy said.

"I'll take you up on seconds anyway," Sophie said, holding her flute up. She wasn't a big drinker, but it was going down smoothly, she wasn't driving, and she needed the liquid courage, considering the topic.

"If you're interested in this firefighter," Betsy said as she trimmed Iona's toenails, "it's better to have the ball in your court."

Though Sophie was a point guard all the way when it came to her business, she was more of a bench warmer in dating, never having taken much initiative in her love life. If a guy made it easy for her and she was interested, she might give him a chance. More often than not, she bypassed involvement altogether. She took three sips of champagne.

"Are you interested?" Iona asked.

Too much.

There wouldn't be a better opportunity to get advice. "Yes." Ddmitting that didn't mean she had to follow their suggestions.

"Hmm." Iona tapped her pursed lips. "Is he working today?" Besty was holding up a sheet of nail color samples, and Iona pointed at a sparkly berry-colored one.

Sophie nodded, and her stomach sank with foreboding that she wasn't going to like what Iona came up with.

"This is going to work perfectly. I have to bake six dozen of my special salted caramel brownies this afternoon for my grand-mother's retirement home—"

"Six dozen?" Besty asked, the nail polish brush suspended a foot above Iona's toes.

"I do it once a month. She loves them. Everybody loves them. Which is why they're the perfect thing to take to the fire station as a token of your thanks." Iona directed the last bit to Sophie.

"My thanks."

"For saving your life," Betsy said.

"Of course."

"Then you run into Nate and ask him out." Iona's eyes shined brightly with enthusiasm.

"I've never asked a guy out," Sophie said, veering more toward dread than enthusiasm.

"Never?" Iona asked.

"Hot firefighter," Betsy said. "No time like the present."

"Pretend it's business. You could ask the president of France to lunch if it were business."

Iona had a point. When it came to engineering and architecture, Sophie had the utmost confidence. She wondered if she could fool herself long enough to pull off asking Nate out. Maybe with another bottle of golden bubbly, or maybe two.

"I don't know how to bake."

"We bake together."

"It's a great plan," Suri said as she held out the same sample-color selection.

Sophie normally wore pastels on her nails — both finger and toe, always self-applied — but she stopped herself before she could point to the shell pink on the second row. "Fire engine red," she said, or rather, the champagne said.

"Theme!" Betsy hollered.

"Are you in?" Iona asked.

Sophie eyed her glass. She tipped it up and finished off the last swallow. She had to admit she didn't like the thought of not knowing when or if she'd see Nate again. Iona's plan was beyond Sophie's comfort level, but she'd cross that bridge, well, in a couple of hours.

"I'm in."

God help her.

9

"Good scald tonight, Ed. The habañeros…" Dylan gave the lieutenant, Nate's dad, a fist bump as he cleared the older man's bowl from the table in the fire station kitchen. "My mouth is on fire, man."

"My chili's not for the weak of heart," Ed Rottinghaus said.

"He doesn't do mild," Nate told Dylan. "He serves the Thanksgiving bird with jalapeños and hot sauce. You gonna join us this year?"

"I just might."

Nate and Dylan shared the cleanup duties tonight since Ed had cooked and most of the other guys on duty had just been called out on a medical. The TV in the corner of the room was on, and Ed turned the sound up on the local news. "Hey, look," he said.

"Officials now believe the cause of the fire to be arson. The office building was a total loss, but the property owner says he plans to rebuild as soon as possible. Investigators have asked anyone who has information regarding the fire to call the hotline at the number on the screen…"

There was no new information in the segment, but Nate had turned off the faucet and set aside the dirty chili pot as soon as it had started. "Hope they catch the bastard," he muttered to himself.

"How's Sophie doing?" Dylan asked. "Have you talked to her?"

"She was released yesterday. She's doing pretty well, all things considered."

Nate heard his dad's chair scrape the floor and knew his old man was now gaping at him, probably with a toothpick sticking out of his mouth. "Son, is there something you aren't telling me? Who's Sophie?"

"Sophie Alexander."

"She's the hottie he carried out of the fire," Dylan said with a knowing grin.

Ed stood and took the empty bread plate to the counter, setting it down next to Nate, who'd resumed washing the large stainless pot. He could feel his dad's gaze fixed on him.

"What?" Nate said, going for innocent because he didn't know what else to do.

"You seem to know an awful lot about this 'hottie.'"

Nate was a grown man, and there was no reason to hide that he'd visited Sophie. More than once. No reason other than avoiding the shit he knew his old man would flip his way.

"I drove her home from the hospital. No big deal."

"You sure that's wise?"

That elicited a laugh from Nate. "Driving her home? I think it worked out okay for everyone."

"Seems above and beyond the call of duty," Ed said.

"And?" Nate said, finally glancing toward his dad, who did, indeed, have a toothpick hanging out.

"Where were you last night?" his dad asked.

Nate met his gaze directly. "At her condo."

Dylan let out a whoop, and Nate thought about punching him to shut him up. Then he realized how out of proportion that reaction was to the situation and shook it off.

"I made her dinner," he said. "That's all. Hell, you were still awake when I got home, old man."

"You made her dinner? Shit," Dylan said, and Nate's dad stared at his son as if he'd just announced he was having a sex change operation.

"I can't remember the last time you cooked a woman dinner," Ed said, turning his back to the counter and leaning against it, arms crossed. "Oh, hold on a sec. I remember. *Never.*"

"Told you she's hot," Dylan said.

"How do you know what she looks like?" Nate asked.

"She was in the newspaper, man."

Nate hadn't thought to check it out, but he would.

"Gotta be careful, son. You'll want to make sure she's not a groupie."

Nate scoffed. "She tried to ditch me when I came to pick her up, Dad."

His dad let out a belly laugh, and of course, Dylan couldn't shut the hell up either. Nate blew them off.

"She sounds like exactly what you need then." Ed nodded, as if he were an expert on anything having to do with women. Of course he'd think he was, since, for the first time since Nate's mom had left, the lieutenant was seeing someone. Seeing an awful lot of her.

"Rotten House!" Rafe Sanchez's voice came from out in the hallway. "Better get out here!"

Nate rinsed off the clean pot and handed it to Dylan to put away. He dried his hands with a paper towel, beaned it at Dylan's head, then went out to see what Rafe was hollering about.

"What the hell do you want, San—"

Sophie was standing in the hall where it intersected with the public entryway.

Nate stopped. Looked around for Rafe as if he could explain, but the medic had vanished.

"Wha— Sophie." He walked toward her, unable to keep the smile off his face. "You're not who I expected to see." Behind him, he heard his father and his blockhead friend craning their necks out of the kitchen. "Go away," he called over his shoulder.

"Sorry to disappoint," Sophie said, looking shy. Nervous. Enticing.

"You're much better-looking than Rafe, trust me." He stopped a foot away and resisted the urge to touch her.

Her cheeks had spots of pink in them today, and her eyes looked more alive. The thin layer of coral-colored gloss she'd put on didn't hurt either. In fact, it made him get caught up looking at her lips for too long. Her voice still had a sexy hint of roughness to it, and he wondered what she'd sound like when she was fully recovered. He selfishly hoped she didn't lose all of the rasp.

"I brought homemade salted caramel brownies for everyone. To say thank you."

He glanced down at the plastic-wrapped oval platter stacked three high with chocolate squares. "Smart, gorgeous, and she bakes, folks. Come with me."

"I don't, actually."

"Don't?"

"Bake. I can run a handheld mixer like nobody's business — if you turn a blind eye to the splatters of chocolate all over the kitchen — but the baking cred goes to my business assistant and friend, Iona. She's your goddess."

"You get at least fifty percent credit for mixing — and delivering." He led her into the kitchen against his better judgment because the two stooges were still hovering, trying to decide what they were more interested in checking out, Sophie or the brownies. "This is Sophie Alexander," Nate said, setting the plate in the center of the table, which was tradition whenever someone brought in something to share. "Sophie, that's Dylan Long" — he pointed to the shorter, younger man who'd practically rushed the table — "and this is my dad, Lieutenant Ed Rottinghaus."

Sophie seemed to freeze when she realized she'd walked into meeting his father, but she covered it almost instantly. "Nice to meet you both. Lieutenant." He stood, and she shook his hand and looked all business. Then she offered her hand to Dylan, who already held a brownie in his left one. "Dylan."

After shaking her hand, Dylan took a bite and groaned as if the dessert was as good as sex. "Amazing."

"I wanted to thank the department for saving my life. These seem a little inadequate…"

"Best thank you for these guys is food," Nate's dad said,

helping himself to one before settling back down in the captain's chair at the head of the long table.

Nate looked from his dad to Dylan, who also settled into a chair. Both of them stuffed chocolate into their mouths and stared at the TV screen, which was now tuned to *Wheel of Fortune*. Neither of them got the idea that maybe they should scram and give him some privacy with Sophie.

"How about a tour? Or a walk?" Or anything to get away from his father and Tweedledee.

"Oh. Sure."

He reached out his arm toward her and pressed his hand to the small of her back, finally giving in to the urge to touch her.

MAYBE SOPHIE WOULD BECOME a nun or something. That had to be easier than asking a good-looking, funny, dripping-with-muscles firefighter out on a date. How had she let Iona convince her it would work out?

Champagne was from the devil.

She wasn't sure about pedicures either, although, underneath her boots and a layer of socks, her fire-engine-red toenails did look good.

Nate showed her the common areas of the station and the sleeping quarters and gave her a quick glance at the offices, and then they headed out to the apparatus floor, as he called it. In her mind, it was the garage. They walked across two vast, empty bays to the truck on the far side. She'd tried to pay close attention to everything Nate had said on the tour, but she got sidetracked easily, by things like his hands, the length of his fingers as he pointed to something, the way his navy blue uniform pants that were supposed to be utilitarian and boring hugged his butt just enough to give her thoughts — non-PG thoughts...

"This here is the hose we pull out for car fires," Nate said at the front of the truck. "It's hooked up and ready to go. Fast."

He led her around to the driver's side, beyond the cab, and opened compartments. Explained what everything was. The smooth timbre of his voice lulled her and made it hard to concentrate on what he was saying. As she stared at him in his white SAIFD T-shirt, uniform pants, and boots, remembering the feel of his short, coarse hair in her fingers when they'd kissed, any confidence she'd built up to ask him out faltered. Maybe she could just make a quick escape and call the brownie delivery good.

"These gauges control all the hoses … the pressure … the… You don't really care about all this, do you?"

"I…" Sophie jerked her gaze to his. "I do. But I was…" So busted. "Trying to work up the nerve to ask you out." It came out in a rush, an ungraceful, uncool rush, but it was out there now.

Nate's look of concern morphed into a half grin, and he stepped closer to her — a lot closer than a tour guide would stand.

"Yeah?" He rested one hand on the side of the truck, his hazel eyes piercing hers, and it seemed like he was interested.

Sophie swallowed. "If I did, what would you say?"

"Well, that depends…"

"On?"

"What'd you have in mind?"

Her plans suddenly seemed lamer than ever. *Business, Sophie. Imagine this is for work.* "Dinner at Raul's," she said, banking on the knowledge that it was one of his favorites, based on their conversation last night.

"Hmm…" He peered down at her, and she fidgeted.

Her pretend-it's-business scheme was flawed. She rarely asked business associates out in person — it was usually planned via email or a phone call. And she *never* stood this close — close enough that she could smell his soap and the salty, spicy maleness that was his scent — when talking to a business associate.

Nate laughed quietly. "I'm torn."

Between yes and no? Sophie tried not to let her panic show on her face.

"I'm torn between watching you try to hide how nervous you are and telling you I was going to ask you out too."

Her shoulders relaxed, and she breathed out. "Cruel."

"Maybe a little. Guys shouldn't have to do all the sweating."

"Maybe not, but I'm glad they do most of it."

Nate brushed her hair behind her shoulder, then ran his fingers over her cheek, making her heart skip a few beats. "A guy would be crazy to say no to you."

She stifled the urge to turn her head just enough to press her lips to his fingers. "Is that a yes?"

"As long as it's more than just dinner. I'd hate for you to go through all this pain and torment just for an hour-and-a-half date. There should be something afterwards."

She could think of a few somethings afterwards, but she didn't have the nerve to say so, even as a joke. His fingers trailed back into her hair, onto her neck, giving her shivers and making her think of being alone with him and his hands and the rest of him. Her body responded with an ache between her legs.

Clearing her throat, she reined her thoughts in. "I came up with dinner, so you get to figure out what's after that. Whatever you want, as long it's doctor approved."

"Doctor approved. So no marathon running. No boxing. No contact sports. I think I can work around those."

She endeavored not to think too hard about contact sports with him. "Friday?" she asked.

"It's a date."

A date had been her objective from the start, so why, as they forgot about the rest of the truck tour and walked back toward the main door, did she feel suddenly sick with nerves?

10

The night had been too good. Better than any other date Sophie had been on, and it hopefully wasn't close to over yet, because there was enough tension between her and Nate — the good kind of tension — that a simple goodnight kiss at her door wasn't what she wanted.

Even the setting was romantic. After their superb, no-frills dinner at Raul's, Nate had whisked her away to their mysterious destination, which turned out to be the miniature golf course overlooking the bay on the south side of the island. Sophie had never been there, as it was usually overrun with tourists, and golf had never been her thing. Oh, who was she kidding? The idea to go mini golfing had never even remotely crossed her mind.

The course was nearly deserted tonight, thanks to temperatures in the fifties and Texans' general tendency to consider anything under seventy-five downright freezing. With a thick sweater and a date who liked to touch her, it was bearable. More than. In fact, fifty degrees might become her new favorite temperature if it meant she got to have Nate's arm around her all the time, with his body pressed next to hers, infusing her with even more than ninety-eight-point-six degrees of heat.

"Do you like your cocoa with whipped cream or without?" Nate asked as he sat down next to her on the picnic bench near the water.

"Without, if I have a choice." She rarely allowed herself to drink cocoa — hello, carb city — but tonight had the feel of a special occasion.

Nate handed her a steaming cup with a cardboard strip around it to protect her fingers from the heat. Their hands touched — for the two hundredth time tonight — and the spark of interest still jolted her, made her long to touch him more.

"Thank you."

Though she'd been marginally interested in the guys she'd dated in the past and she'd had sex with a couple of them, this was different somehow. She'd never been this attracted to a man before, never ever in her life considered inviting a guy to come home with *her*. They seemed in tune with each other, like Nate was as into her as she was him. There was a connection there, something she couldn't put into words. Something she couldn't allow herself to think about too hard.

It'd been a couple of years — okay, more than three — since she'd been on a date. Maybe this was just the difference between twenty-eight and thirty-one years old. Weren't women supposed to be at their sexual peak in their thirties?

"Still can't get over it that you've never played mini golf before," Nate said as he wrapped his arm around her waist, pulled her into him so that their bodies touched all along their sides, from their thighs to their shoulders. "Or that you won that first game."

"I was close on the third game, don't forget. Next time, I will prevail."

"Beginner's luck."

"Never." Sophie laughed. "I may be more than a little competitive."

"I thought you were going to ask them to turn the background music off so you could concentrate on that last shot."

"Hey, a free game was at stake. That would obligate you to take me out again."

Nate turned his head toward her and nuzzled in close. "That's the kind of obligation I can get behind. But if you think free golf is a requirement for me to take you out again, you're missing some serious signs from me."

He glanced over his shoulder toward the bright lights of the course, then nodded toward the city walkway in front of them that wound along the shore all the way from the southern tip of the island to the bridge that crossed to the mainland. "Want to take a walk? Get away from the tinny-sounding music pumping through those crappy speakers behind us?"

She took a sip of her cocoa and nodded. She wanted nothing more than to be alone with him. He stood and held out his hand, and she took it with her empty one. They locked their fingers together, the roughness of his skin giving her an inexplicable thrill.

As they put distance between themselves and the blaring, treble-heavy music, the night became quieter. Peaceful. Nothing but the two of them. There was a slight breeze, but this side of the island was protected and much calmer than the gulf side. Nate's hand and his attention warmed her to her toes anyway.

They finished their cocoa and threw the cups away in a trash can along the path.

"It was good, but not nearly as good as the brownies you brought to the station," Nate said. "My dad said to tell you those were the best brownies he's ever had, and he's had a lot of brownies in fifty-five years."

Sophie laughed. "I'm telling you again, I had very little to do with how they turned out. But I'll give the message to Iona." Without discussing it, they turned onto a wide dock and walked out over the water to a bench at the end. "Your dad seems nice. Quiet though."

"He was just behaving himself for once. He's rarely quiet — at the station or at home."

"You work with him *and* live with him?"

"Yeah, as much as I hate to own up to living at home. I have the top floor, he has the bottom, and the middle is the living room and kitchen. It's a bachelor pad through and through."

"Big-screen TV?"

"Yep."

"Pool table?"

He laughed. "In the family room."

"You're living a stereotype."

"I know. It's not so bad, but I'm thinking it's about time for me to get my own place," he said. "Lately, it's gotten weird. My dad has a lady friend. First time since my mom left."

"Sounds … tricky."

"Yeah, nothing like running into her in the kitchen at six a.m., me in my boxers and her in a robe."

"Awkward."

"I'm just relieved she was wearing a robe. Thanksgiving will be strange this year. Our tradition is to totally bachelor out. We fry a turkey, make a full-on feast, and invite any guys from the station who don't have family nearby. Football on the TV, pool games ongoing. This year, Elsa will be there."

"Do you like her?"

"I don't really know her. He's just started bringing her home within the past two weeks."

A fish jumped a few feet out from the dock, and without thinking, Sophie rested her head on Nate's shoulder, breathing in the night air. Savoring the contentment.

"You should join us for Turkey Day if you don't have other plans. Then it wouldn't be so weird."

Sophie lifted her head, alarmed. Thanksgiving? With his family?

"Um, I … I don't really do Thanksgiving, but thank you. If Elsa gets along with your dad," she said, rushing on in an attempt to divert his attention from her refusal, "I imagine she'll hold her own with any of the guys who show up. It sounds like you two are close enough you can weather a lady friend. Thanksgiving or otherwise."

The way his look lingered at her from the side told her he'd noticed. She held her breath, waiting for him to pursue her reasons for saying no to his invitation.

"Yeah. Don't get me wrong — I'm happy for him. Just gonna take some getting used to it. It's been the two of us for so long…"

"How long?" Sophie asked, breathing again. Diverting his

attention again.

"My mom left when I was nine. Third grade. Crushed me. She sat me down one night before bed and told me she was 'called to help.' She left on her first missionary trip to Costa Rica two days later, and every day after that, for God knows how long, I used to run all the way home from school to see if she'd changed her mind and come back yet."

"She didn't?"

"There were visits every once in a while. They became less and less frequent. I got older and madder, and when I was sixteen, I told her I didn't want to see her anymore."

Sophie's chest tightened with an all-too-familiar ache. She battled it, tamped down the anger that always came with it, this time on his behalf as well as hers.

Not now. Not on this perfect date.

Managing a squeeze of support on his thigh, she discreetly turned her head away, as if the headlights of the cars crossing the mile-long bridge in the distance had caught her attention. In truth, she didn't want him to see if her eyes glistened suspiciously.

"I'll never understand how a person can just walk away from her family," he said. "Her kid. *Her own flesh and blood.* You know?"

God yes.

She stood, as if the view of the water in the dark was better from two feet closer, when she was really fighting hard against everything inside of her that was trying to get out.

Nate came up next to her. Didn't touch her except where his upper arm barely brushed her shoulder. "I guess ... yeah. Maybe you do know?" he said.

Jaw clamped tightly, she bit down on her tongue, zeroing in on the physical pain because *that* she was in control of. That she could handle. The tempest inside caught her off guard — it'd been ages since she'd allowed the feelings to invade this much. Ages for everything except the anger, because getting mad was easy.

"How old were you when your dad left?" Nate asked quietly.

No. She wasn't going there. Wasn't answering that question, because then there'd be another … and another. And all of the answers would rip her open little by little.

Her pulse pounded in her throat and at her temples, and she sucked in the cool night air slowly, discreetly. Deeply. Willed the pounding to ease and frantically tried to come up with a way to avoid this topic that she'd never gone into with anyone.

"Sophie?" Again, he wove their fingers together.

She turned toward him, looked up at his handsome, shadowed face. His eyes that stared questioningly back at hers. His lips. Standing on tiptoe, she kissed him, eager to taste him again and, yes, eager to distract him.

Within seconds, she was distracted herself, caught up in the warmth of his breath, the taste of his tongue, the feel of his hand on the back of her neck, gentle at first, then drawing her closer. Her senses were overcome with him, the hint of chocolate on his breath, the heat of his hands and his mouth, the quiet sounds he made as they explored and caressed each other.

NATE WAS TORN. On the one hand, he wanted to kiss this woman for a month or so without stopping. On the other, he wasn't an idiot. He could read signs, and he was getting a big, fat disconnect on the conversation he'd tried to have.

He'd always been a big fan of compromising, which was why he spent a good few minutes devouring her mouth and relishing her sweet taste, her sexy little noises. Each time they came up for air, he tried to convince himself to pull back, but it took several attempts.

"Soph," he finally said, still nibbling at her delectable lips.

"Yes?" Her voice was a sexy purr.

"Don't think I didn't notice that."

"Notice what?"

By sheer force of will, he took a half a step back so their bodies were no longer touching. He entwined their fingers, both hands, and leaned his forehead into hers, unable to break the connection fully. "The way you dodged that conversation. About your dad," he said gently.

After witnessing the phone call from the guy the other day in the hospital, Nate was curious as hell. Mystified that she was so hateful of him. Sophie didn't seem like a hateful person. Admittedly, he didn't know her very well in some ways, but in others, he felt like he'd known her for years. And that only made him want to understand the story between her and her father that much more. She must have good reasons for feeling the way she did. It was an unfamiliar thing — wanting to understand every single facet of this woman and her life. Foreign territory for a guy who'd always been content to play the field and avoid getting hooked at all costs.

Seemed he'd gotten hooked the second he'd seen her terrified, determined brown eyes in the fire.

"I... Yeah," she said. "I don't talk about him." There was no apology in her voice whatsoever.

Nate nudged her chin upward with his fingers so she met his gaze. "I want to know you, Sophie." He bit down on anything else that might pop out of his mouth. He didn't want to freak her out, and frankly, his feelings were freaking him out more than a little.

"You've seen me at my worst," she said with a half grin. "That's more than ninety-nine percent of people ever get to know."

He couldn't make himself smile back. And yet he couldn't say what he wanted to. He'd like to avoid the label of creeper at all costs.

"Nate, we met less than ten days ago. I'm not good at this. Opening up—"

"I get it." He nodded, knowing she was right. "It's okay."

Nate bent forward and pressed his lips to her forehead, battling the maelstrom inside of him. He was losing it. It was whacked out to care so much about someone so fast. Someone who wasn't wild about letting him care, letting him know her.

"It's okay," he repeated, "but I should probably get you home."

11

"Thanks again for allowing me to come with you," Nate said to Chief Mendoza as the two of them and Penn Griffin, the arson investigator on the case, rode the elevator up to Sophie's floor Tuesday evening.

"It's not the norm," the chief said.

"She doesn't have anyone who's really there for her," Nate said.

"No family?" Penn asked.

"Not that she talks about." Of course, she hadn't mentioned the brother, and Nate was still trying to swallow her lack of trust in him.

Small fish, he decided as the doors opened and the three of them stepped out.

The chief knocked on Sophie's door. Nate stood off to the side and tried to prepare himself to lay his eyes on her again. It'd been four days. They'd texted a few times since their date Friday that had ended on a … well, not a particularly high note. Just casual messages, a half dozen in total. He was smart enough to realize when he'd been coming on too strong. And yet he had to be here for this.

The door opened and Nate's heart hammered. It'd taken all his willpower to stay away from her for ninety-six hours. He drank in the sight of her. Her hair was pulled sloppily back, with several pieces hanging down and framing her face. She wore black yoga pants and another heavy zip-up sweatshirt that hit her mid-thigh. Her eyes turned warier than usual when they landed on the chief and Penn, but he thought she warmed a few degrees when she spotted him. Wishful thinking?

"Hello again, Chief Mendoza, Penn. Hi, Nate. What can I do for you?"

"Can we come in, Sophie?" Chief Mendoza said. "There's been a development."

Sophie's eyes veered to Nate's, and he wanted to pull her close, tell her everything was going to be okay.

"Of course." She stood to the side and let the chief and Penn walk in. Nate paused next to her, rubbed her upper arm. "What's going on?" she asked him in a quiet voice.

Nate nodded at the other two. "They'll explain. I'm just along for the ride."

"Have a seat," she told the others.

Chief Mendoza and Penn seated themselves on opposite ends of the gray couch. Sophie went to the adjacent love seat, and Nate sat next to her, several inches away, on the edge of the cushion.

"Is there a new lead in the case?" Sophie asked.

Penn and the chief exchanged glances. Chief Mendoza nodded, giving Penn the go-ahead, and Penn cleared his throat.

"More than a lead, Sophie. There's been a confession."

Her eyes widened, but that was her only reaction. No, Nate decided as he watched her with hawk-like focus. Not the only reaction. She was holding her breath, waiting. He put his hand on her thigh to convey his support, suspecting she was going to be blindsided.

"A man came in earlier today and admitted to starting the fire at the office building on Garcia Avenue."

She pressed her lips together, moistening them, and her eyes darted to Nate for a moment. "Why? Why did he do it?"

"He claims he didn't know anyone was in the building when he started the fire," Penn said. "He was going for property damage, apparently. Shock value, as well, in my opinion." Penn paused, and Nate tensed, knowing what was coming. "Sophie, the man who confessed is Robert Alexander."

"*What?*" She grabbed Nate's hand, dug her nails into his skin. Her face turned ashen, looking like she had right after the fire. "My brother?" When she glanced at Nate, she explained, "Estranged. I haven't talked to him for years."

Nate nodded, signaling that he wasn't worried she hadn't mentioned him — at least not at the moment. If Robert Alexander was the kind of guy to torch his sister's office, Nate could understand why she'd neglected to talk about him. It did make him even more curious about her family's history, but he shoved that aside.

"He didn't know you were inside," Penn repeated.

"That doesn't make it okay!" Sophie stood and took several steps.

"No," Chief Mendoza said, his voice quiet and yet still conveying the passionate hatred that everyone in their profession held for arsonists. "It's not okay."

"So he wanted to burn my office down, didn't he?" she asked, her back to them as she gazed out the window toward the Gulf of Mexico.

"It appears he's got a lot of issues," Penn said. "Resentment, anger…"

Sophie laughed harshly. "You think?" She wrapped her arms around herself, as if protecting herself from memories.

"That guy is overflowing with jealousy. It seems he's jealous of everything about you, though that's not quite how he phrased it."

"I've worked my ass off for everything I have. While he was getting suspended from school and picked up for shooting BBs at local businesses' windows, I was studying. Working. Doing something with my life."

Nate walked over to her. "There's no way to make sense of a person like that, Sophie."

She dragged in a ragged breath.

"He's in custody now, so he won't hurt you," Penn said from behind them.

She nodded vaguely, lost in thought. Nate rubbed a hand back and forth on her back until she turned away from the window and faced the others.

"Is there anything else I need to know right now?" she asked.

Penn stood. "Just that we'll be doing everything in our power to see that he gets the maximum punishment." His voice held determination. "And again, he's behind bars now. You're safe."

She bobbed her head again, looking a little more alive, a little less shell-shocked. "I appreciate you coming over to update me," Sophie said to Penn and the chief. "You too, Nate."

"I'm not going anywhere," he said. "I'll find a ride home later."

The chief sized him up and gave his silent consent, and Sophie didn't protest.

"We'll be in touch soon, as we work on the case, Sophie," Penn said. "I'm sorry to have to deliver such disturbing news."

"It's a lot to digest," she said as she led him and the chief to the door.

"It sounds like this isn't the first sign of trouble from your brother," Penn said.

Again, Sophie laughed, but it, too, was far from her normal laugh. "Oh, no. Not the first sign. Thank you, gentlemen. I appreciate your visit."

Nate narrowed his eyes at the change in her tone. It was like she'd become all business and they were discussing a building remodel or something, not a murderous, sick-in-the-head family member.

They said their good-byes, and Sophie closed the door and leaned against it, allowing the all-business act to fall by the wayside.

Thank God, because that was going to piss him off. Nobody could get news that a sibling had almost killed him or her and not be bothered.

But still, he was walking a fine line between being the support she needed and … too much.

Still slumping against the door, she pressed both her hands to her face, covering her mouth and nose. Nate walked toward her, but she didn't even notice.

"Come here," he said, pulling her into his arms.

She came to him willingly. Hands still covering her face, she burrowed into his chest. Nate breathed in her scent and felt centered. Content. The need to give her the same feeling pulsed through him, but he wasn't sure how.

"It's gonna be okay," he whispered. He kissed the top of her head and tightened his arms around her, imagining what he'd do to her brother if he ever laid eyes on him. The bastard was lucky to be locked up, frankly.

Most women he knew would be bawling right about now, but he didn't feel so much as a shudder of her shoulders ... for better or worse. He wasn't well versed in the art of comforting a crying woman, but with the news she'd just gotten, she should be doing something besides standing there frozen. Shouldn't she?

"Sophie? Talk to me, darlin'. You breathing?"

A few seconds later, he felt her nod. She removed her hands from her face and wound them around him. Held on for all she was worth. Which was just fine by him. He was glad to have any kind of response, especially one that wasn't pushing him away.

They stood there for eons, not talking, the only movement that of his hands caressing her back. "Tell me what you need," he said. "What can I do?"

In response, she shook her head. A few seconds later, she straightened. "Can we go outside?"

"On the balcony?"

Sophie nodded.

He took her hand and walked toward the door. On the way, he snagged the blanket from the back of the easy chair.

Outside, the two teak lounge chairs stood sentinel over the view, which was now shrouded in darkness. Purposely not turning on the outdoor light, Nate sat on the one in the corner, the most protected from the wind, and pulled Sophie down crosswise on his lap. Once she was settled, he draped the blanket around her shoulders. She tucked her head into his shoulder, her hand resting on his chest.

They sat like that for several minutes, not speaking, the roar of the waves insulating them from the rest of the world. Nate had so many questions about her brother, but he didn't want to infringe on any calmness she'd found since the chief and Penn had left. It wasn't time for talking yet, unless she started it. He could be patient.

Sophie curled in closer to Nate, if that was possible.

The news from the arson investigator had caught her off guard, but honestly, when she thought about it, wasn't really shocking at all. Her brother was a loose cannon. Always had been. Though she wasn't aware of any record of him doing something on this scale, he'd always been on the edge, like he was just one rage away from blowing up the world.

The fear of him was so old, so much a fundamental part of who she was, that there was no grieving for what he'd done to her. Mostly, now that the facts had started to sink in, there was … profound relief. She hadn't realized it before, but now it was clear as day that, on some level, she'd always been waiting for Robert's crazy to surface somehow, sometime. Always. Even though he hadn't been in her life for years and years and she hadn't laid eyes on him for more than a decade. Didn't matter. She'd always known that he and his brand of crazy were out there somewhere.

Now he wasn't. Or not free, anyway. He was in custody, and hopefully he'd be put away for a long time. At any rate, Sophie would breathe easier.

Was she pissed? On some level, she felt fury, but she didn't have the energy for it. Robert Alexander wasn't worth it. So she pushed any anger aside, maybe for another time. Maybe for never. She'd learned early on that getting angry was letting him win, because getting a rise out of people was part of what her brother thrived on.

Not today. She wasn't going to give in to it. Honestly, she just wanted to forget it. Forget him.

With one finger, she traced a line up Nate's ridged chest and back down, over the faded red cotton of his T-shirt. His body was a perfect male specimen, like a model for a drawing class where the challenge was to show all the ripples of muscle and valleys between and arcs of perfection. The only drawing she ever did was for building schemes and plans, with lots of straight lines and angles, but she imagined sketching his masculine beauty as she continued to explore his chest and shoulders.

His strong, scruffy jaw was next, and she relished the texture under the pad of her finger and tried to commit the exact curve to memory. She was drawn to the contrasting smoothness of his lips and hesitated only a moment before running her finger over the bottom one and then the top. He opened them slightly, as if to say something. Sophie traced another circle over them, her heart rate picking up, and she finally got the nerve to lean in and press her mouth to his, gently. Their breaths mingled, and then she traced the same path with her tongue, lightly, teasing his lips.

"Sophie." His voice was a low rumble, barely more than a whisper. "You must be reeling…"

She toyed with his lips a moment more before answering. She had no desire to talk about her criminal, psychopathic brother. Brushing her knuckles over his jawline, she shook her head. "I'm okay."

"Do you want to talk about…?"

"No. I don't want to waste a single second on him. He's so one thousand percent not worth it."

She pulled his head back to hers and kissed him again, less gently, more insistently, trying to communicate without words. She managed to distract him for a minute or so before he broke contact and spoke again.

"I came with the chief and Penn to be here for you, Soph, but this doesn't feel like what we should be doing."

A wave of self-doubt rolled through her, and she straightened. "You don't like me kissing you?"

His lips flirted with a grin. "I always like you kissing me, but you just found out—"

"Please, Nate."

He brushed her hair away from her face, running his fingers over her cheek and then cradling her jaw. His milk-caramel eyes stared back into hers, searching.

Maybe it wasn't normal of her to not be in hysterics over tonight's news. Maybe it was crazy that she wanted to distract herself from everything with this beautiful man. There was nothing normal about her situation or the way she'd lived in constrained fear for practically her whole life.

"Tell me what you want, Sophie. What you need…"

She swallowed, knowing full well what she wanted but unsure whether she had the nerve to ask for it.

Screw it. No more fear.

She shifted so one leg was on each side of his thighs and her body was centered over his, and it was impossible to miss that, regardless of his protests, his body was hard as stone and good to go.

"I want you to make me forget the rest of the world exists."

12

N ate could only fight his reaction to Sophie for so long.

Her beautiful eyes, the ones he'd been entranced by since the very first moment he'd seen her, gazed down into his. Implored him.

He rested his hands at her narrow waist just above the outward curve of her soft, feminine hips. His thumbs nearly met in the middle of her flat abdomen. He was surrounded by her softness and struck by the determination in her eyes when he looked back up at her.

She'd just told him, in essence, she wanted sex, and he was hesitating *why*? Doing the "honorable" thing only went so far. At this point, in this situation, it verged on stupid.

Nate had always endeavored not to be stupid.

He reached up to the zipper of her sweatshirt and eased it down all the way, revealing a plain, salmon-colored tank beneath, no bra, and nipples that had definitely gotten the message he intended to grant her wishes.

Now that he'd let his defenses down and decided to give in to what he wanted, what she'd asked for, it was as if his self-control had taken a hike. He lifted the bottom of her tank and ran both his hands over the warm, smooth skin on her abdomen for a moment before raising them to palm her breasts. Perfect, more-than-a-handful, luscious breasts with large, rose-colored nipples.

Nate had to taste them. He toyed with one nipple with his tongue before pulling the tip into his mouth selfishly, hungrily. The way Sophie ground her pelvis into him and moaned told him his selfishness was working pretty well for her too.

While he laved one breast with his tongue, he explored with the other with his fingers, circling the tip, rolling it between his finger and thumb, palming the sweet weight of it. Sophie exhaled with a shiver.

"Should we move inside?" he asked as he adjusted the fuzzy blanket over her back and shoulders.

"I'm not cold. Nowhere near it," she purred. Glancing over her shoulder toward the beach, she continued, "The beach is deserted tonight, and no one can see us from below anyway. Unless you prefer going inside…"

They could be smack dab in the center of the beach in broad daylight or in the middle of rush-hour traffic, and at this precise moment, he still wouldn't be able to get her clothes off quickly enough for his tastes. "I'm fine." Times one hundred.

She pushed his shirt up his chest, and he helped her raise it over his head and drop it to the balcony floor. He kissed her thoroughly, pulling her head to his and running his other hand up and down her gorgeous, softly curved body. His jeans constricted him to the point of pain, and he shifted beneath her, causing more glorious friction and eliciting another soft, sexy moan from her. God, he couldn't wait to watch her come.

Nate slid his hands under the waistband of her yoga pants and worked them down as far as he could, which wasn't far, due to the way they were sitting. Leaning first to one side and then the other, Sophie helped him, until she straddled him in nothing but a wispy, aqua-blue pair of bikini panties. Ignoring the discomfort in his own jeans, he slid his body down in the lounger and guided her to rise onto her knees.

"What…?"

He pressed his lips to her core, over her thin panties, and she gasped. Held on to the back of the chair behind his head. Looked down at him through lust-filled, heavy lids, and that elicited a growl from deep in his chest.

He teased her with his tongue on top of the silky material, his fingers working beneath, and the smell of her arousal reached him. She was wet for him, writhing for him, and it was so fucking hot.

Moving the underwear to the side, he slid his tongue home to her opening, and Sophie moaned. He reached down to unfasten his own pants, hoping to ease the discomfort, but the way she moved over him, into him, his blood pounded through him and centered in his cock. She was killing him, but he was determined to give her what she needed before sliding inside of her.

"Oh, God, Nate," she said and repeated that and variations of it as he worked her over with his tongue and fingers. After some time, her body arched into him, tensed, and the graphic words that came out of her sweet mouth nearly made him lose it.

She wilted into him, and Nate pushed himself back up in the chair, then wrapped his arms around her, pulled her into his chest.

"That qualifies," Sophie said with a sated half grin.

"For?"

"Forgetting the rest of the world exists."

A sparkle appeared in her eyes, and then she sought out his neck with her mouth, nibbling him, licking, kissing, working her way up to his ear and just below it, driving him mad. Because he just wasn't turned on enough.

Yeah, right.

She trailed a path downward, over his jaw, to his chest, at the same time going to work on his jeans, inching them lower. He helped himself to her breasts again, molding them with his hands, rasping his thumbs over the nipples, thinking this was about as close to heaven as a guy could get.

Nate raised his hips to help her get his jeans down just enough that they were out of the way, and then he felt her palm close around his cock. He leaned his head back and bit his lip. She stroked him, caressed him, made his eyes roll back.

He felt like a fucking adolescent, but he said it anyway: "Soph, if you keep that up, I'm not gonna last long…"

Her wicked grin told him she loved his struggle.

Still grasping him, she moved, pushing the thin strip of her panties aside and teasing his tip with her slick, swollen opening.

Nate ran his hands up her rib cage to her breasts, attempting to divert her. Failing. "Soph..."

"Yeah?" she said, her voice whispering directly into his ear.

"We should use something."

Her breath came out in a shudder, as if she was ready to go again and *into* this.

"I'm on the pill," she managed. "And clean..."

He nodded and sent a prayer of thanks to whoever was listening. "Same. Well ... the clean part."

Sophie let out a shaky laugh. "Okay, then."

She slid him inside of her, sheathing him tightly, drawing a low, primal moan from him. Eyes closed, she didn't immediately move. Nate tried to calm the fuck down and reel himself in before he embarrassed himself.

With her hair draping over both of them, she grinded and pivoted her hips, her breasts bouncing front and center. Nate knew the erotic image would be imprinted on his brain forever. He grabbed the globes of her ass and held on, bucking with her movements, losing his mind and matching her intensity as it increased to a fevered pitch.

"I've never ... come ... more than once," she said, throwing her head back, her breathing shallow and uneven.

"No time like the present, darlin'," he managed.

She arched her back and moaned his name and a stream of other things, and that was all she wrote. Nate thrust into her and came for all he was worth.

Breathing hard, Sophie collapsed onto his chest, reaching to pull the blanket over her shoulders. Nate wrapped his arms around her and held her, registering the sound of the surf and the chill in the air for the first time in several minutes. Her sweet scent enveloped him as her hair fell over his cheek.

"That wasn't what I was thinking when I admired this balcony before, but I gotta say I like it even more now." He pressed a kiss to her cheek.

Sophie smiled lazily and turned her head to look at him. "Your open-mindedness is admirable."

"Flexibility is a virtue, right? We seem to make a good, flexible team. I'd say a twelve on a scale of ten. At least."

"I'm afraid I'm out of practice."

He laughed, a low, satisfied sound. "You can practice on me anytime, darlin'."

The breeze picked up momentarily, and with the sweaty sheen covering both of them, it had a chilly edge to it.

"How do you feel about shooting for a thirteen out of ten in a hot shower?" he asked, thinking it'd be even more stupendous to have her fully naked this time.

She shifted on his lap and reached between them, to his semi-hard cock, making it stiffen more. "Really?"

"I wouldn't lie about such matters," he said.

"I like to think I'm generally up for a challenge. And there is that competitive side of me."

"I was banking on it." Nate sat up straight, wound his hands beneath her amazing ass, braced a leg on either side of the lounger, and stood with her in his arms. "So how do you feel about coming three times or more in one night?"

13

The number was more than five by the time Sophie and Nate were tangled up, naked, in her bed under the blankets. She rested her head on his chest, listening to his heartbeat.

She was practically buzzing from the attention he'd given her body and slightly dazed with fatigue, but she couldn't ignore the faint uneasiness starting to jab at her, trying to wipe out all the good stuff of the past few hours.

Though she tried not to let it filter into her consciousness, it wasn't hard to figure out the cause: She'd never allowed a man in her bed. Definitely never let a man stay all night at her place. The very few men she'd slept with before had been elsewhere — at their apartments, hotels, whatever. Purposely not her home.

You brought this on yourself by starting everything when all he wanted to do was make sure you were okay.

Truly, it was damn difficult to regret *starting everything* when it had been so … well, *amazing* didn't quite cover it. Amazing times a hundred.

Nate played with her hair, idly twisting it around his finger, and the gentle motions soothed her further, helped her shove aside the underlying apprehension.

"When I convinced Penn and the chief to let me come with

them tonight, this was not my intention, I promise," he said. "But I like the way it turned out."

"Me too."

He turned onto his side, pulling her flush against him and upward enough so their heads faced each other on the pillow. "I want to know you better, Sophie."

She laughed nervously. "I'd say you got to know me quite a bit better tonight."

He didn't laugh at her attempt at a joke. "I wish you would trust me enough to open up about things."

Her heart sped up, and not at all in a good way, the way it'd done earlier. "I've never been a very open person. It's not easy."

"I get that. Well, kind of. But there's nothing you could tell me about your brother or your family, for example, that would change the way I feel about you."

Her gut tightened. "It's not that I think you would judge me. It's just … private stuff."

She could see the narrowing of his eyes in the dim, moonlit room. "I'm trying not to push. Trying not to let it bother me."

But it did bother him. Obviously. No matter what he said or how he tried to accept it, he wanted her to tell him about the fucked-up dynamics of the Alexander family, among other things.

"It's … hard," she said. "Too…" She shook her head. Too emotional. Painful. Made her doubt everything about herself. She was so not going down that road tonight or anytime soon. Honestly, there were just some subjects she didn't talk about. Ever. She never had. Letting them out now would give them power. Discussing them would let in all the horrible feelings — doubt, sadness, disappointment, fear. Fear that she wasn't enough…

Nate watched her patiently, clearly not understanding. After several seconds of silence, he rolled to his back. Disappointed. In her. In her shortcomings. Even though he was trying not to show it, Sophie could feel it coming off him.

There was very little she hated worse than being a disappointment.

"We haven't known each other for long," she said, knowing the argument was weak.

He nodded. "I know."

Sophie rolled away and closed her eyes. He was trying to be patient. Trying not to push her. And she could probably put him off till a later date — maybe next time they were together, maybe even a month from now.

But what it came down to was that she wasn't comfortable with opening up to someone that much, with allowing someone that close. She didn't know if she ever would be.

She bit down on the piercing frustration — frustration with everything. With him for needing what she couldn't handle, with herself for being so fundamentally closed off, with the situation … because she'd gotten a sample of something so good, and it ultimately wasn't going to work out.

Damn. It. All.

The backs of her eyes burned with tears she would not shed. She already cared about Nate more than she'd cared about anybody before. Squeezing her eyes tightly, she felt like pounding the mattress, throwing a tantrum.

None of that would help though. Because there was no getting around the truth: Losing him now was going to hurt. But losing him later would shred her to pieces.

Inhaling a deep, fortifying breath, she gathered her courage, forced the tears away, and barreled ahead with the only thing she could do.

"I … I don't think this is going to work," she said, sitting up on the far edge of the bed, swinging her feet to the floor so her back was to him.

"What?" She heard him roll toward her. "Sophie…"

She stood and grabbed her silk robe that hung over the footboard and wrapped it around her, wishing it could shield her from sadness.

The bed springs squeaked as he bolted out of the other side of the bed. "I wasn't saying—"

"I know, Nate. I do. You're not pushing me. You're trying hard. But what you don't understand is that this is the kind of person I am deep down inside. Always have been, since ... forever. *I'm* the problem. I wish I weren't. But the issue isn't going to go away. It'll only get worse. And the closer we get, the more nights like tonight we share ... it would just be that much harder."

"I'm willing to give you time, Sophie," he said as he walked around to her side of the bed. He stopped in front of her and exhaled, as if the look on her face had let out all his steam and he'd lost momentum. He brushed her hair behind her ear and cupped the back of her head.

Sophie looked up at him, at those eyes that spoke to her like nothing, like no one else. If she couldn't make it work with him... They'd known each other a short time, as she'd said, but they'd been through a lot already. He'd sneaked in past some of her defenses. Part of that was because of how they'd met, because of what had happened to her. This man had been there for her in the hospital when nobody else had, and she'd been weak, physically and emotionally, and let him in further than she was usually comfortable with.

If she couldn't make it work with him, chances were she wouldn't be able to make it work with anyone, now or in the future.

Maybe she wasn't trying hard enough. How big of a deal was it, really, to just give him what he wanted? Why not tell him all her secrets? Why not let him *really* know who she was and what she came from?

Panic seized her, and the bedroom walls seemed to close in at the thought.

Yeah. That was why. She was too much of a coward.

"Time won't help, Nate. I'm not the kind of woman you're looking for, and I'm sorry. I really, really wish I was." She turned away and went to her dresser to dig out some clean clothes, barely able to see through the tears. "I'll drive you home."

"You're serious, aren't you?" he said, the first hint of anger seeping into his voice. "You're going to take an amazing night, an amazing couple of weeks, and throw it away because you're scared."

"Yep," she said, keeping her voice matter-of-fact, because really, he'd summed it up perfectly.

He swore and turned away, took a few steps, and picked up his jeans off the chair where he'd set his clothes. He yanked them on as she pulled on clean underwear and leggings.

"You know what kills me the most?" he asked. "The thing that attracted me to you from the first moment…" He shook his head and sucked in a loud breath as if steadying himself. "The thing that drew me in was your courage. The determination I saw in your eyes the instant I shined a light in them in the middle of a raging fucking fire. What happened to that, Sophie? Where's that courage now?"

She swallowed hard, his words hitting a little too close to home. Right smack in the center of her. It took a gargantuan effort to keep her voice even, unaffected. "I guess it was false advertising."

And *this* was exactly why she didn't let people know her better. Because the person she was deep down, the one no one really knew, was never good enough for love.

Sophie pulled out the thickest sweatshirt she owned and zipped it up to her chin, but it did nothing to comfort her. "I'll get my keys."

As she walked past him, he reached out and grabbed her arm, stopping her. They looked at each other for several eternal seconds until she broke eye contact, hating the hurt she saw in his, hating even more that she was the cause of it.

"Don't worry about it," he said. "I'll call a friend." He whipped his shirt over his head.

"I said I'd give you a ride home—"

"I've got it covered. Good-bye, Sophie."

14

Sophie was *not* going to Iona's the next day to whine about her failed-before-it-really-started relationship with Nate.

She'd had to escape from her condo early that morning. The walls had been closing in on her all day, and all night too, ever since Nate had left. She'd gone to the dojo and convinced Jack to work with her for her first krav maga workout since the fire, but even that hadn't helped. Trying to work at home today, the day before Thanksgiving — which was really her only option since she didn't yet have a new office for Green Systems — had proven futile. Everywhere she looked, she saw Nate. He'd been to her place exactly twice, and yet he'd been in every room, infiltrated each one with memories, and right now, Sophie couldn't handle those. She only wanted to forget.

After ringing Iona's doorbell, Sophie took in the details of the tiny, well-kept adobe house tucked into a modest neighborhood on the mainland. This was the first time she'd been to her assistant's house in the almost three years Iona had worked for her. And her visit had nothing to do with work. She was here because she once again craved friendship.

The door opened, and Iona's welcoming smile gave her the sudden urge to cry.

"Come in," Iona said, arms open for a hug.

Sophie went to her with only a moment's hesitation before realizing a hug was exactly what she needed.

"Thanks for letting me barge in," Sophie said, holding on to her friend for an extra moment to try to dry her eyes. "I brought beverages." She handed Iona the bottle of Shiraz she'd picked up on the way over.

"The best kind of beverages. Thank you. I'll pour us a glass." She led the way down a short hall to an old-fashioned, compact, bright yellow kitchen with a built-in dinette. "Have a seat."

"How soon are you leaving for Thanksgiving?" Sophie asked as she slid onto the wooden bench.

"Not till tomorrow. Noonish. Two-hour drive, and my family goes out to a restaurant for dinner every year so that nobody has to slave over a stove."

"Going out on Thanksgiving sounds nice."

"That's what happens with five brothers who don't cook, only one of whom is married." Iona worked with a corkscrew for several seconds before the cork popped out. "If my mom were still with us and I weren't the only girl, everyone would bring a dish and no one would think it's a big deal. Boys are nothing but a pain in the butt. Double pains in the butt when they become men."

The tears Sophie had forced back seconds earlier reared their heads again. She looked down, opened her purse, and pretended to search for something, anything, so that Iona wouldn't notice. She spotted the unopened travel pack of tissues and went after one. "Stupid men," she managed without her voice giving her away.

Iona set two full glasses of wine on the table, then settled into the seat across from her. She lifted her glass, presumably to offer a toast, but froze when Sophie met her eyes. "Sophie, what's wrong?"

Sophie blew out all the air in her lungs. "Damn."

Iona set her glass down and put her hand over Sophie's. "Tell me."

Sophie's lip quivered, and she fought to get it under control. "This isn't why I came over…"

"It's okay."

"Or maybe it is. I hate this." She dabbed at the corners of her eyes with a tissue.

"I have cookies. This looks like cookies might be required. How about if I get those while you work out what you want to say."

"Cookies," Sophie said, about to remind Iona she didn't eat cookies. "Bring 'em on."

When Iona sat back down, Sophie had taken several warm, calming sips of wine and felt like she might be able to speak without losing it.

"Chocolate chip, gingerbread, and scotcheroos."

"You baked these?" Sophie picked up a scotcheroo and savored the first heavenly bite.

"For Thanksgiving. Because even though we go out, there's always a time and place for homemade cookies. Now what's going on, Sophie? You can tell me."

Sophie took another bite first. And another. Because this homemade cookie was one thousand times better than talking about herself. When Iona leaned forward to stare accusingly into her eyes, she swallowed her carbs and sat up straighter.

"I ended it with Nate," she said in a rush, before she could get all closed-throat again.

Iona stopped chewing mid-bite, her eyes going huge. "Firefighter Nate?"

The way she said it, scandalized, as if to say *who would ever break up with a firefighter*, almost made Sophie grin. "The one and only."

"Shit, Soph. Forget cookies. I can see if I have tequila." She started to get up, but Sophie stopped her.

"It's okay. It's for the best. My condo was just … mocking me."

"Times like those, living alone sucks."

Sophie nodded, astounded by how well this woman got her. And just having someone understand … well, strangely enough, it helped.

"I'm so glad you came over. Now tell me all about it. What happened?"

Three more sips later, Sophie decided what the hell. She told her most of the story, skipping over her brother's confession — because that was mostly irrelevant — and sex details. It was embarrassing enough to admit they'd done the deed multiple times.

"Okay, let me make sure I've got it straight. Sex was fantabulous?"

"And then some."

"But then afterward, there was a role reversal, and he wanted to talk, but you didn't?"

Sophie grinned weakly. "Pretty much."

"But he backed off."

"Yes. For now. But…"

"That'll only last for so long. Because, Sophie, honey, he's into you. He wants to know everything there is to know about you."

Just hearing the words made Sophie squirm. "And therein lies the problem."

"You don't think you could ever talk about your family?"

"I don't talk about my family. They're dead to me." Or they had been until they'd tried to make *her* dead. Stuffing them back into that category was proving difficult.

"Bad stuff?" Iona asked, a sympathetic look on her face, and Sophie answered with a nod.

Iona refilled their mostly empty glasses. "We all have skeletons, Soph. Stuff we hate. Stuff we hate to admit to. Every last one of us."

"Maybe." Brothers who tried to kill their sisters, not so much. Dads who cared so little about their kids that they were able to walk away without looking back and move on to a new family, not so much.

"Tell me something, Sophie. Be honest with me. What are you afraid of?"

"I'm not afraid." Even as she said it, she knew it was a lie.

But Iona didn't call her on it. If she had, it might've been easier to argue, to convince both of them she wasn't scared. Instead, her friend took a silent sip of wine and waited.

Having emptied her second glass enough that it wouldn't spill, Sophie spun it around by the stem. "Maybe I am," she conceded quietly.

"Maybe?" Iona's question was gentle. Sympathetic.

"For sure." There wasn't enough wine in the world to make this not suck.

Iona touched her hand again — she was more touchy-feely than Sophie had ever realized — and leaned forward. "News flash, Sophie. When it comes to love, everybody's scared. Love is scary."

"I didn't say a word about love."

"Potential love. If that potential wasn't there, you wouldn't be here right now."

Again, Sophie couldn't argue. Her knee bounced up and down, and she broke a cookie into bite-sized pieces and stuck them into her mouth one by one.

"Are you afraid of losing a guy you care about?" Iona asked.

"Well … of course." Because, yeah, she cared. In the past, she hadn't worried about it because there hadn't been a guy she'd felt particularly strongly about. By her design, no doubt.

"And you think talking about things that are important to you will scare Nate away?"

"I guess so."

"Sophie, I don't know a lot about your family either, but if this guy is as crazy about you as he sounds, then I don't think you have anything to worry about."

"Maybe you're right." Sophie pursed her lips and shook her head.

"That's not enough to convince you, huh?" Iona said with a sad smile. "Maybe the timing just isn't right for you two."

"Maybe." Which was still a big bucket of suck. "I'll get over it," she said, sitting up straighter. "Thanks for hearing me out. I really didn't come over here to go on about him. I want to hear about something happier. Like that little baby boy your brother's wife just had."

"I have a new picture," Iona said, perking up and pulling her phone out. "Cutest. Thing. Ever." She flipped through photos with her thumb, then handed over the phone to Sophie.

It was a professional studio shot of the family of three. Iona's pretty sister-in-law sat holding the tiny baby, who was decked out in a darling baseball outfit, and pressed her lips to the little guy's forehead while Daddy stood behind them. But what really struck Sophie was the look of utter love and adoration in the man's eyes as he stared at the mother of his son.

The knot of sadness balled up in Sophie's throat again and pulsed with every beat of her heart. *That's* what she was missing out on if she couldn't just get over herself and open up to the right man someday.

The problem was ... what if Nate happened to be that right man?

15

Thanksgiving was just another workday for Sophie, with the exception of letting herself sleep in for as long as she wanted to before she got down to business. That's why she was confused when she awoke to someone ringing her doorbell … again.

Her first thought was of Nate, but there was no way it was him, she knew. Iona was the only other person who might be out and about on a holiday and who knew where she lived.

The condo was chilly, so Sophie threw on a sweatshirt over her pajama pants and camisole. As she hurried to the door, she twisted her hair through an elastic band to the back of her head. Glancing toward the kitchen on her way, she figured she could whip up some scrambled eggs and toast for an impromptu Thanksgiving brunch if Iona stayed for a while.

She opened the door without looking — a mistake she'd learn to never make again.

"Oh," she said, stopping short.

"Sophie, don't slam the door, please," her father said. He held out a bouquet of light pink tulips. "May I come in?"

Sophie stared at him for seconds, dumbfounded. She scowled and started to close the door.

"Sweetheart, wait." He held a hand out against the door, stopping her.

"First thing, do not call me sweetheart. Second thing, how the hell did you find out where I live?"

He looked up and down the hallway. "It wasn't that hard to track down. Could I please come in for fifteen minutes? Then if you want me to leave, I will."

She stared at the thinning dark hair that matched the color of hers, at the lines that traversed his face — no laugh lines or crinkles from smiling too much — and saw a weary, old, unfamiliar man.

"Fine. Fifteen minutes." There was no *if*. He *would* leave the second his time was up.

She opened the door and stood back, wishing herself a happy fucking Thanksgiving.

"Where to?" he asked, gazing around her apartment like a spy.

"Right here's fine."

He held up the flowers. "Got a vase?"

She didn't want anything that would remind her of him, but skipping the argument would get him out of here faster. She took the bunch and slapped them onto the pass-through to the kitchen.

"Sophie," he said when she turned back around, "I am the world's worst father."

She leaned against the wall and crossed her arms over her chest.

"I owe you an apology."

"I stopped waiting for anything you might owe me years ago," she said, not bothering to hide the bitterness from her tone.

"I deserve that." He nodded. "I don't blame you for hating me, but I'm wondering ... I'd like to try to earn your forgiveness."

He looked at her imploringly, and she merely raised her brows. Being such a bitch was almost uncomfortable, but this was the father who'd deserted her family, she reminded herself. The father who had turned his back yet again, for the last time, two weeks after her mother had died, when Sophie had dropped every last bit of her pride and asked him for help paying for college. Had money been the issue, she would've held it against him less, but his reason had been that he had a new family and hadn't wanted to "rock the boat," as he'd said.

"You can't earn forgiveness," she said.

"Well, I sure can't get it without apologizing, so I'd like to start there. Sophie, I am sorry as hell for the way you grew up. I'm so, so sorry I never took your brother's problems seriously."

After all these years… She'd waited for *so long* for her dad to acknowledge any kind of problem, even before he'd walked out on the family. For as long as she could remember, she'd been the afterthought. Her brother had been the attention hog, with their mother tirelessly trying to get him psychological help and her father endlessly belittling her mother for being unable to handle a "rowdy, attention-seeking boy."

There'd been a time, eons ago, when his apology would have changed things for her, but now … it was so little and so very, very late. Her heart had hardened, and she couldn't just thaw it on a moment's notice.

"You thought Mom was nuts," she pointed out.

"I couldn't acknowledge that my son, a child who came from my genetics, might have serious problems. I can see now that's due to my own insecurity, but Sophie, after figuring out what he did to you—"

"What do you mean, figuring out? He confessed."

"He confessed because I essentially caught him red-handed."

"How so?"

He moistened his lips nervously. "Are you sure you don't want to sit down?"

"One hundred percent sure. Just tell me."

He looked around helplessly, then ran his fingers through his thin hair as he sighed. "He's been staying at my place for about a month—"

"He's been living with you?" As far as Sophie knew, their dad had washed his hands of both of his children as soon as he'd left.

"He stays there sometimes. When he doesn't have anywhere else to land, I guess. He's quite the drifter. I don't ask questions.

When Lorie left me, the place got too big and lonely. I was glad to have the company—"

"Your time's ticking," Sophie said.

"The night of the fire, Robert came home in the middle of the night. Which is nothing out of the ordinary. But a couple days later, I noticed the clothes he'd thrown in the laundry room smelled like heavy smoke. I didn't put the pieces together until several days later when I noticed the gas can for the lawn mower was missing from the top of my workbench in the garage."

"So you confronted him and he confessed?" she asked doubtfully. Her brother had never been one to make things easy.

"Not exactly. But eventually I took him in, and he told the investigators everything. Listening to him, I finally saw what your mom saw all those years. Things are plugged in wrong in his head."

That was a pretty accurate way to put it. Too bad it came two decades too late.

Sophie gritted her teeth together, unsure whether her anger was sparked more by her brother or her father right now.

"Why'd he do it?" she asked. "They said he didn't know I was in the building."

"Well…" Her father rubbed his chin and looked at the floor.

"The investigator said he's jealous, but that's just stupid."

"He's full of hate, Sophie. His life isn't good, and that's a lot his doing, but that man harbors so many bad feelings. Some are my fault, no doubt. If I could do anything to turn back time and change everything—"

"You can't."

"I will regret the way I treated you for the rest of my life. Your mother was right in her never-ending search for answers, for help for Robert. But because I didn't see it, he could have killed you."

"I have a hard time believing that would matter to you."

His head sank to his chest, and there was no mistaking his shame.

Sophie couldn't deny a tiny bit of gratification, but she didn't want to think about what that said about her. She'd tried so hard to move on, to get over not just his lack of love but his total disregard for his own daughter, but obviously she still had emotional scars.

"I'm not a good person, Sophie. I've got nothing. Nobody. And it's my fault completely."

"What happened to your new family?" she asked. "When I called after Mom died, you told me you couldn't help me because your new wife was pregnant and wouldn't understand."

"Lorie probably would've understood if I'd helped you. She was a much better person than me."

"Did she die?"

"She divorced me. Rightfully so." He straightened, as if summoning the last bit of dignity he possessed. "I'm not here for your sympathy. I just wanted to tell you that what Robert did to you ... it chills me to the bone. I'm ashamed that it took such an irrevocable action on his part for me to see the truth. And again, I'm sorry."

"So what do you want from me exactly?" she asked.

He studied her for so long she became antsy. Finally, he shook his head. "Just wanted you to know I'm genuinely sorry." There was nothing in his stance or his face that said he had an ulterior motive, and he looked so empty, so beaten down that she almost felt sorry for him. Almost.

"I want nothing for you but happiness," he said. He glanced around the condo again. "But I suspect maybe you don't have that yet, otherwise you wouldn't be alone on Thanksgiving, like me."

That did it.

"Go. Get out of my house. What I do and what I have is no business of yours."

"I didn't mean that as a shot at you, swee— Sophie. I truly don't want you to end up like me. Alone. You've got so much going for you — look at your career. I couldn't be prouder of you. For someone to survive the kind of childhood inflicted on you..." He shook his head. "You're special, Sophie. And I'd like to believe you're going to be okay, but..." He gestured to the empty condo. "It's a holiday, and you're as lonely as I am."

Clenching her jaw so hard she thought she might chip a tooth, she marched to the door, opened it, and waited for him to leave.

Her father lifted his chin and arched his neck back in defeat. "I haven't handled this right at all, but then I imagine neither of us is surprised." He glanced at the tulips that lay scattered across the pass-through, no longer neatly arranged, then hiked up his pants and walked to the door. "Happy Thanksgiving, Sophie."

She met his eyes with a glare in an attempt to convey all the years of feeling unloved, unlovable. It took every bit of willpower she had to shut the door quietly, calmly, when she felt anything but calm inside.

Leaning her forehead against the closed door, she breathed in, willing her body not to collapse like a tower of blocks when someone kicked it.

When she felt steadier, she walked to the refrigerator, opened it, took out the half-full bottle of chardonnay, got a glass down from the cabinet, and stopped with the bottle tilted over the glass.

No.

She put the glass away, set the bottle back in the fridge.

Drinking away her loneliness was *not* the answer. That would make her no different from her father. And dammit, what he'd said had hit too close to the truth.

She wasn't happy. And maybe part of that was because she was alone. Maybe a big part.

That, of course, brought Nate to mind. He was never far from it anyway.

The last time her father had called, when she'd still been in the hospital recovering, Nate had been with her. She closed her eyes and remembered what it'd felt like to have him offer his silent, nonjudgmental support. His touch on her shoulder had been so simple and so … exactly what she'd needed, whether she'd been able to see it then or not.

It occurred to her at that moment that the bad stuff was less bad, a little easier to handle, when you didn't have to handle it alone. When you had someone who cared. Someone who you cared about.

She'd spent so much of her life, so much effort convincing herself that *alone* was how she wanted to be, to keep from getting hurt or let down again, but from the moment she'd found herself in the fire, facing the possibility of death alone, it'd become harder to believe in.

Sophie was alone, she realized, chiefly because of the people who'd been unable to love her the way she needed to be loved — her mom to some extent, but even more so, her father. For almost twenty years now, maybe more, she'd lived in fear of not being lovable, but the problem was *him*.

She didn't want to be alone anymore, and that was in large part because there was someone she wanted to be with badly enough to try.

The instant the thought coalesced, she jumped into action, pushing herself away from the kitchen counter and checking the clock on the microwave. Just after eleven a.m. She tracked down her cell phone in her purse and punched a number from her contacts.

"Iona, hi, it's me. Are you still in town?"

"Hey, Sophie. Happy Thanksgiving! I was just getting ready to load up the car. What's up?"

"I have a baking emergency of sorts. I was wondering if I could have your caramel brownie recipe ... and, since the grocery store's closed today, maybe you have the ingredients?"

It turned out Elsa, Nate's dad's lady friend, was okay.

She was a bigger football fan than anyone, if fandom could be judged by loudness and yelling at the refs. Nate grinned in the kitchen, where he was rinsing off some of the dirty dishes, as, in the living room, she explained to the ref exactly what pass interference was and told him to keep his goddamn eyes open for it.

Dinner had been okay too. Tasty turkey, decent sides, good desserts. It was all okay. And yet the day was lacking.

"Rotten House, you bringing in the rest of that cheesecake?" Dylan hollered from the recliner he hadn't moved his ass from since kickoff.

Nate overlooked the demand. If Dylan hadn't shown up today, Nate would've been the third wheel, big-time. And while Elsa was nice enough and Nate and his dad were close, sitting through the holiday with the two lovebirds would've been hell.

How the mighty of the San Amaro Island Fire Department had fallen. Five years ago, the Rottinghauses had had their biggest crowd on Turkey Day with seventeen. Seemed like, since then, everyone and his dog had hooked up, gotten married, some of them with kids, even, and now he could add his dad to the list of the "attached."

He picked up the plate with the store-bought cheesecake and

grabbed the pumpkin cookies Elsa had baked as well and took them out to the living room. Setting them on the coffee table, he verified that the score of the game hadn't changed and then headed back toward the kitchen.

"You not gonna watch the end of the game?" his dad asked, his arm around his ever-swearing lady and his feet perched on the ottoman.

"I think the Cowboys have it in hand." They were up by twenty-four with less than ten minutes remaining. "Gonna start cleaning. You people made a mess."

Dylan tossed a wadded-up napkin at him and slid another piece of cheesecake onto his plate. "I'd help you but I'm still eating."

Nate waved him off. He wasn't in the mood for company anyway.

Thanksgiving was usually one of his favorite holidays, but this year, something was off. Not something, someone. Him. He knew the reason, and he hated it. He was sitting around pining the fuck away for a woman who wanted nothing to do with him.

It pissed him off because, first off, he wasn't that kind of guy. He'd never cared enough about a woman before to get bent out of shape. Second off, he was still upset that Sophie was too scared — of who knew what — to give them a chance. So close and yet … so over.

Shit. What a waste of a Thanksgiving. Since when did he need more than a fried bird and a football game to have a good holiday?

As he soaped up the overflowing dishwasher, he heard a knock at the front door. Probably some of the guys from the station stopping by on their way home from a family celebration.

"Hey, Sophie," he heard Dylan say from the other room, and Nate poured about twice as much soap in the receptacle as necessary.

What the fuck?

Heart hammering, Nate closed the dishwasher and pushed the appropriate buttons, his ear tuned in to the other room. It was entirely possible Dylan was messing with him. He wasn't going to go in unless he heard Sophie herself.

And there was her voice, saying hello to his dad, greeting Elsa as she was introduced.

Nate froze. What was she doing here? He blew out a breath and went to the doorway to the living room.

Without a word, he feasted his eyes on her. She looked more beautiful than ever — or rather, more dolled up than ever, because she was always beautiful, whether covered with black soot or just rolling out of bed — with her hair cascading in wide curls down her back and over her shoulders, shimmery copper eye shadow that deepened the brown of her eyes, a soft-looking pale pink skirt that hit her midway up her gorgeous, toned thighs, and a sexy, gauzy cream-colored shirt. She wore knee-high brown leather boots and a jacket that matched.

Nate had to remind himself how they'd left things. How she'd kicked him out of her condo. "What are you doing here?"

"I..." She took a few steps toward him, looking unsure. "I baked brownies. By myself, this time, so don't get too excited because apparently there's a learning curve. But they should be edible. Sort of." She held out the covered pan, and Dylan swooped in. "Eat at your own risk," she said.

"Stomach of steel," Dylan told her and helped himself.

"No idea where you're putting all that food," Nate said to his friend, and to Sophie, "I'll put them in the kitchen."

He didn't know what to say, so he said nothing and went to the kitchen. Sophie excused herself from the others and followed him in.

Nate set the pan of brownies down and frowned. The ones she'd brought to the station had had a trail of caramel artfully twisting over the top. These ... well, artful wasn't the word he'd use. They were dark around the edges. Definitely well done. But the aroma of fudge — and a little bit of burnt sugar — wafted up to his nostrils.

"As I told you," she said, "my first time. They're not perfect."

"I was just wondering how I could fit any more food in. So..." He tossed the dish towel draped over his shoulder to the plate-covered counter, leaned against the oven, and crossed his arms. "I thought you didn't do Thanksgiving."

"I… Yeah… I haven't in the past." She raised her gaze to his, and he felt it deep in his gut. "I … think I've been missing out."

"A holiday of eating. Doesn't get much better than that. How'd you find out where I live?"

She looked at the floor. "I'm not at liberty to say."

"Firefighters are a sorry lot. They'll do just about anything for a pretty face."

"Are you saying I'm pretty?"

Was she flirting with him? He resisted the impulse to flirt back because then he'd feel like an idiot if she shot him down again and walked out the door in five minutes. "You know I think you're pretty, Sophie. Why are you here?"

"I… I'd like to talk to you."

He looked closely at her and saw fear. Insecurity. And any reluctance he'd had to hearing her out trickled right on out the door. Coming here to talk to him was hard for her.

"Can we, um, go somewhere private?" she asked, looking over her shoulder toward the living room.

The others were caught up in the game again, but that'd be over any minute and then they'd trundle out to the kitchen for more food. "Let's go upstairs."

He led her up the narrow flight of stairs to his part of the house, a large studio-like room with his bed, a couch, TV and video game system, weights, and a desk with his ancient computer on it. Several moving boxes were piled up in the corner, half full, as he'd started the search for his own place. The room was not exactly neat. Had he known Sophie was coming over, he would've spent some time making it look better.

He grabbed a blanket from the couch and then opened the door on the long wall that led to the world's smallest excuse for a balcony. Sophie followed him out.

"This thing doesn't meet code, in case you were wondering," he said as he sat on the edge of the platform and dangled his feet between two of the vertical posts that supported the railing. He dropped down to the shallowly slanted roof of the kitchen below, which he considered his private, railing-less balcony. As Sophie came down after him, he spread the blanket over the rough shingles to protect her bare legs.

They both sat down, keeping several inches between them.

"Do you have a view in daylight?" she asked, squinting in the direction of the shore.

He leaned toward her and pointed. "Between those two buildings, you can usually see some waves."

"Nice."

"Said the girl with the oceanfront condo."

"Luckily, somebody made me see how lucky I was before it was too late."

"Somebody, huh?"

"Yeah. Somebody who made me see quite a few things, actually."

He narrowed his eyes at her, trying to determine her meaning, but she kept her gaze straight ahead.

"Nate … I'm not sure where to start, but I have lots to say."

Cautious optimism started to take root deep inside. He tried to keep it in check because she could mean anything. But the fact that she'd tracked down his address, baked him brownies — shared the imperfection of her brownies with him, at that — and seemed willing to talk…

She scooted closer to him and folded the outside edge of the blanket over her legs, supporting her weight on her hands behind her.

"My dad showed up at my condo this morning."

"How'd that go?" he asked carefully.

"Oh, probably about as good as you might guess. He apologized for being an awful father. Et cetera, et cetera."

Nate tried to imagine how it would be if his mom showed up out of nowhere and took full responsibility — and blame — for failing him and his dad. While she'd popped in from time to time when he was younger, it'd never been to apologize. At least not genuinely.

That'd take some absorbing, at the very least, he guessed.

"Was he? An awful father? I mean, I guess it's obvious he must've been for you to hate him, but…"

"But you don't really know because I haven't told you anything."

"Well, yeah. But don't feel like you have to—"

She sat up and pulled her knees to her chest. "I want to." She darted a look at him. "Okay, that's maybe not entirely true, but I *need* to. I'm ready to. I've never talked about my family to anyone before, partly due to not liking to talk about them, but also partly due to not having anyone to tell. Nobody who really pushed me. Nobody who truly wanted to know."

"Every family has a dark side, Sophie. They all look so normal from the outside, but they're never normal. Normal doesn't exist."

"I kind of know that. It's not that I think mine is so much worse than everyone else's…"

"Then what?"

She shrugged. "Mine is personal, I guess." She attempted a laugh. "I walked away from my family… No. That's not true at all. My dad walked away from me. My brother was always a wild card, and my mom died of cancer."

"So really, they all kind of deserted you," Nate said, moving closer to her and taking her hand, understanding how significant it was for her to confide in him.

"My dad did. Absolutely."

Losing her mom at eighteen had to have been infinitely hard as well. Barely a legal adult. He hated to think about losing his dad.

Sophie took a slow, audible inhale and closed her eyes before continuing. "Some of my earliest memories are of waiting rooms in psychologists' offices. For my brother. We spent hours in them. Sometimes multiple times a week. My mom would pack up my coloring books and a box of crayons, a pile of picture books, and my favorite stuffed animals to keep me occupied."

"What's wrong with your brother?"

She scoffed. "Question of the hour. Oppositional Defiance Disorder, Borderline Personality Disorder, several other possibilities were thrown around. My mom was determined to find a way to help him. Determined or … obsessed."

"But not your dad?"

She shook her head. "That's how their marriage ended. He insisted Robert was just a boy with a lot of pent-up energy, too much time on his hands, too much boredom. My mom knew it was more."

"Based on your brother's recent activities, it sounds like your mom was right."

"My parents fought all the time. It was horrible. And then Robert was always getting in trouble. For as long as I remember. He got suspended, expelled, changed schools, started new treatments until the new doc would say they'd done as much as they could, usually because of lack of cooperation on Robert's part. Chasing answers was all my mom did until my dad left."

"What'd she do then?"

"She had to go to work. She held down two jobs to try to pay for all the therapy, which my dad refused to help with."

"Dedicated."

Sophie pursed her lips together. "It ruled her life, really, the pursuit of answers for Robert. Ruled *our* lives."

A surge of protectiveness engulfed him, like nothing he'd ever felt before. How could these people be so blind to a little girl's needs? "How much younger than Robert are you?"

"Four years."

"You were a little girl, and your mom spent all her time on a crusade for your brother, and your dad … he left. Is that right?"

She smiled sadly. "Pretty much."

"Did you and your brother ever get along?"

"He hated me. I was scared of him."

Nate understood, finally, how she'd had to turn inward. Why she kept everything to herself.

No one had ever been there for her.

"That's all pretty messed up," he said. "*They* are messed up, Sophie. Not you. You are … unbelievably normal, considering what you've lived through."

She laughed sadly. "You said yourself normal doesn't exist."

He slipped his arm around her and pulled her to his side. "Let's upgrade it from normal to amazing."

Her expression became somber. "No. I'm not. I'm… It wasn't my dad's apology that hit me hardest today," she said. "It was something he pointed out."

"Such as?"

"He compared me to him." She said it as if it was the absolute worst insult a person could give, and he realized, in her eyes, it probably was. "He pointed out how I'm lonely and unhappy just like him." Her voice cracked. She took a moment to recover before going on. "I don't want to be like him. But he's right. I spend holidays by myself. Friday nights by myself. Almost every waking hour I'm not working by myself. And while my job makes me happy, my life doesn't. Because … I'm scared."

"Of what?"

Big pause.

"My brother hated me from the moment I was born just because I existed. I was never enough to drag my mom's attention away from my brother's problems. Wasn't enough to keep my dad from leaving…" She inhaled shakily and put her hands over her face. "So how … how could I ever be enough for someone else to c-care about?"

His chest literally hurt for her. "Come here," he whispered. He lay back on the roof and pulled her flush on top of him so they were forehead to chin, thigh to thigh. He wrapped his arms around her and held her tight, and she finally rested her head on his shoulder. As he rubbed her back, up and down, he felt her relax a bit.

***

Sophie let herself melt into Nate, soaking in his warmth and, even more, his acceptance.

"Sophie?" he said, his voice quiet, rough.

"Yeah?" She held her breath and focused on the soothing motion of his hand on her back until it stopped.

He angled his head to make eye contact with her. "You are so much more than *enough*." He stared intently at her as if willing her to believe it, and with his beautiful, sincere eyes penetrating her to her soul, she thought maybe she could. She thought maybe she could be enough for him. Foibles and insecurities and imperfect baking skills and all. She knew she wanted to be.

Nate relaxed back down again and kissed the top of her head. "I know you're thinking I haven't known you very long, but here's the thing. I've known you through some difficult times, and I've known you long enough to figure out I care about you. More than I've cared about any other woman."

His admission did things to her. Warmed her. Calmed her. Filled her with gratitude and … hope.

"I get it, Nate," she said. She closed her eyes tightly, wanting to say more, more than she ever had to anyone, willing herself to do it. She raised herself up so to a sitting position, straddling his hips, knowing this was too big to mumble into his chest. "I get it because I feel the same way."

"Thank God." He sat up with her still on top of him, winding his arms back around her, and she did the same. "I'll be honest. It scares the hell out of me."

He leaned in until their lips met. Their kiss was urgent, needy, not just a physical thing, though that was there too … there and in the hardness pressing between her legs.

"Scares me too, but … well, you already saved my life," she said, grinning, "so rescuing me from myself should be easier."

He growled out a laugh and kissed her nose. "I think I'm up for that challenge."

Sophie squirmed, pressing her pelvis into him. "You're definitely up for something…"

She kissed him again, and this time it escalated quickly to scorching hot. When Nate broke away, they were both breathing hard.

"Too bad there's a house full of people in there," he said.

Nibbling at his lip, she said, "I do know a place with a killer balcony and a comfortable bed, among other things."

"Perfect. Lead the way."

"Not so fast. I'm thinking it might not be the best idea for you to leave your own party."

His shoulders drooped. "You're right. How about if we make a deal. You come downstairs with me. Eat some food, shoot the shit, charm my dad. And then … in return, I'll spend the rest of the night helping you celebrate your first official Thanksgiving. We can *celebrate* till dawn if you want to."

"I like the sound of that … as long as this is the first of many holidays you help me celebrate."

"Definitely the first of many. I tried a holiday without you earlier today, and it stunk."

"It was my brownies that made it, wasn't it?"

"The brownies." He laughed and kissed her again. "If the brownies come with the woman, I'll happily devour the whole pan. But Sophie?"

"Yes?"

"Maybe for Christmas we can bake them together."

IMPULSE

AN ISLAND FIRE SHORT STORY

ABOUT IMPULSE

One mistake could derail his promising future.

Wild nights are a thing of Dr. Sawyer Culver's past—and a rare thing, at that. So why, when he's on the verge of finally doing his family proud, does he make his most impulsive mistake yet with Mariah?

Salsa dancer Mariah Jackson lives to the beat of her own drum. A self-professed flirt, she's never been one to set her sights on any specific man. Until Sawyer bursts into her life...and her bedroom. Now it's up to her to convince him to embrace the life he really wants.

1

____

D r. Sawyer Culver woke up lacking three things Sunday
morning: any solid recollection of the past ten hours,
every last shred of his dignity, and his boxer briefs.

This realization came to him before he could even open his
eyes.

He lay there without stirring — afraid to move, truth be told.
His head throbbed with a sharp, ice-pick pain at the temples and
base of his skull. His mouth was so dry his teeth stuck to his lips,
and his tongue felt like a dirty sock wedged inside of it. Every
inch of his body ached as if he'd run a marathon yesterday.

As soon as he could summon the courage, he cracked one eye
open in hopes of figuring out where he was, groaning against the
bright beam of sunlight that nailed him directly from a skylight
above. An unfamiliar low-slung white shelving unit loomed a
couple feet away from him, away from the bed he, naked as the
day he'd been born, was apparently lying on. The top shelf was
cluttered with so much random crap it made his head hurt more
— a sloppy stack of library books, various pieces of clothing
(some of them distractingly lacy), a white teddy bear wearing
ballet slippers and holding a pink heart that said MY GIRL...

A woman's bedroom.

He closed his eye to the scene and waited for relief. None
came, of course.

Sawyer racked his pounding, dehydrated brain for a glimmer of anything concerning last night and an explanation for why he could suddenly relate to what a dying fish that'd washed up onshore must feel like.

His little sister's wedding had been yesterday afternoon. Rachel had swept Cale, her firefighter groom, away on a surprise honeymoon midafternoon. Sawyer had been fine at that point. Maybe a little buzzed off the wine and champagne that had flowed freely, but he'd been fully cognizant of the goofy grins stuck on the bride's and groom's faces. Matter of fact, it was that palpable happiness he'd enthusiastically drunk his first shot to with a fair number of San Amaro Island's bravest.

Those fucking firefighters could drink.

Tequila. The good stuff. None of that cheap crap that made a man grimace as it went down. *Smooooth.* Too damn smooth.

He lay there unmoving, slowly cataloguing snippets from the evening in an attempt to piece it all together. To figure out the last thing he could remember.

Mariah.

Mariah Jackson, the groom's sexy, salsa-dancing sister. Her face came to mind at the same time he felt movement beside him.

Ah, shit.

Chancing a turn of his head and a look to his left, he confirmed. Mariah. Curled up on the other side of the suddenly small double bed, sound asleep. A lock of her ginger hair was strewn across the mattress just inches from Sawyer's face. Damn redheads...he'd always had a serious *thing* for them. Stifling a groan, he turned his head and his naked body away, hoping when he looked back he'd find himself alone. That he and Mariah hadn't really … whatever they'd done.

What *had* they done? Why couldn't he remember jack shit? Had someone spiked one of his many drinks?

But he could acknowledge the truth. No one had needed to screw with him or his drink. He'd done this to himself.

He had a vague memory of the wedding party and guests relocating from Rachel and Cale's bayside home, where the ceremony and reception had taken place, to Ruiz's Restaurante, best known for its fish tacos, with its ass-kicking margaritas a close second. He didn't think there was a dance floor at the restaurant, but he had a strong suspicion Mariah had tried to teach him the tango. Another flash came to him of walking Mariah to her place in the dark. Talking in her kitchen, her sitting across from him on the counter, her long dancer's legs tantalizing him. Even with his eyes closed now, he remembered her legs.

But as for her bedroom, his memory registered exactly nothing.

He turned his head back to the left, to Mariah, who hadn't miraculously vanished into thin air. Nor had she woken up.

He'd met her a few years ago, when his other sister, Noelle, had been dating Cale. Mariah had been young then, too young, in her early twenties, and he'd been too in the midst of establishing his career in surgery to give any serious consideration to ever thinking of her as more than Cale's little sister.

It'd been almost three years since Noelle's death, and for the longest time, Rachel, Noelle's twin, had fought any feelings she had for her twin's fiancé out of respect...and what she'd eventually admitted was guilt. Thank God she'd gotten over all of that, and now, as of yesterday, this woman beside him was his sister's sister-in-law.

Weren't they just a twisted, mixed-up couple of families?

Baaad decision, dude, he told himself.

Mariah had really caught his attention, not for the first time, two nights ago at the wedding rehearsal, when he'd taken his place as Cale's best man. Mariah had been the maid of honor.

Welcome to my cliché romance novel.

Against his better judgment, Sawyer found himself studying her profile, the delicate features. Her narrow face matched her willowy body. Russet-colored brows arched in a gentle point above closed eyes. Big, animated, green eyes, he remembered. Her nose was thin and unremarkable, which allowed a man's attention to veer to her lips. The top one was thin and formed an alluring bow over the fuller bottom one. Intriguing lips he had no recollection of kissing.

Surely he'd remember kissing lips like Mariah's. Wouldn't he?

Dammit!

He was thirty-six years old. An intelligent, well-respected surgeon who was up for a new job at a larger hospital on the mainland. He'd interviewed for the medical director of surgery position just last week. His wild days — and he had had a few doozies before and during med school — were long over. It was unacceptable to wake up like this. Without a clue about what he'd done in the past ten to twelve hours. He had responsibilities that didn't allow him to be off his game because of a hangover, for one, or sidetracked by a one-night stand, for another.

Responsibilities and a golf date.

Shit, shit, shit.

A golf date with, among others, Dr. Ramon Tennyson, one of the key decision makers for the medical director job. Not to mention, a good friend of his mother. His dear, well-meaning mother, who had introduced Sawyer to Dr. Tennyson and had informed him of the job opening in the first place. What would she think if he blew it today?

He wasn't going to blow it today even if it killed him. Which, gauging the pain in his head, it might.

Panicked, he raised his wrist so he could see his watch. It was 6:57 a.m. He'd be in no damn condition to hit the golf course in an hour if he didn't get the hell up, take an ice-cold shower, and down enough coffee to chase away any lingering tequila from his blood. He ran his hand over his face, trying to wipe away the haziness.

Mariah rolled toward him, making a sexy, sleepy sound, and he held his breath. The corners of her tempting lips curved upward, but she didn't open her eyes. The sheet was twisted around her waist. She wore a shiny dark red Forty-Niners jersey, and the mesh material ignited Sawyer's imagination. He could sort of make out her breasts beneath the fabric. Full breasts with rosy nipples that he wished like hell he remembered. His pulse picked up and throbbed in his now alert cock.

He eased himself out of bed as gently as possible. He looked down to verify that Mariah slumbered on, and he couldn't help noticing the blankets had shifted when he'd gotten up, revealing a dainty, translucent pair of skimpy panties with pink flowers on them ... with Mariah's slender body inside of them.

Swallowing hard, he ignored his headache and glanced around for his underwear and a bathroom. He spotted his tuxedo pants strewn on the floor and picked them up. No boxer briefs.

The first door he tried was a closet, but the next one was indeed the facilities, and lo and behold, there were his wrinkled, white tuxedo shirt and the plain white tee he'd worn underneath.

Still no underwear.

The mirror reflected a sorry-ass sight — his normally sloppy hair veering toward horror-movie awful, his chin and cheeks darkened with the stubbled growth of the last twenty-four hours. His brown eyes were drawn and bloodshot with dark shadows below. He ought to grab a shower — an ice-cold one for multiple reasons — before he faced up to Mariah, but it felt like an imposition on this woman he barely knew.

Barely knew.

The sick feeling in his gut intensified, and it had nothing to do with alcohol.

He wasn't the type of guy who did one-night stands anymore. Had never been particularly big on them, though his past wasn't perfect. But now... He shook his head. He was old enough to know better, about both the alcohol and the woman.

He owed her an apology. Evidently she'd been on board with whatever had happened between them, but that didn't mean he was okay with it. With his decisions.

Sawyer had always been capable of going with the flow even when faced with the unexpected. It was that inherent ability that had him deciding screw the underwear and pulling on his pants commando. The T-shirt was next. He wadded the tux shirt into a tight ball in his fist.

After settling for splashing some cold water on his face with one hand — and stifling a few choice swear words at the shock of it — he dried off, straightened, and opened the bathroom door to face up to the alluring redhead in the bed. He'd wake her up and say he was sorry for acting like a hormone-crazed college kid, keeping his distance the whole time, and then smile and get the hell out. Except...

Damn it all.

In yet another unproud moment, he couldn't get his legs to cooperate. Couldn't bring himself to take the five strides to the bedside and rouse her. The door to escape the bedroom was closer, and without deliberation, he went through it and walked out of her apartment.

2

Sawyer Culver was a looker, no question about it.

Mariah awoke with his beautiful face in her mind — and a gut feeling that he was no longer next to her in bed. Bummer. Maybe if she didn't actually look, she could pretend he was still there. She rolled to her side away from where he'd slept, keeping her eyes closed. Her leg veered backward to his spot a little bit, just to be sure.

Yep, gone.

For now.

She remembered the first time she'd met him, four or five years ago, when her brother had taken her to dinner to meet his then-girlfriend's family. It was tough to forget meeting a man who looked like Sawyer with his just-scruffy-enough-to-make-a-woman's-jaw-drop good looks with eyes that were intelligent enough that one could easily buy in to his respected-surgeon role as well.

The whisper in her head that sounded simply like *yesss* whenever she interacted with him had only begun this weekend as she'd had the opportunity to talk to him more, get to know the man behind the growl-worthy exterior. All it had taken for Mariah to fall for him was a few hours of discovering the contradictions that were Sawyer: the rough-edged appearance with the charming yet sincere personality; the touch of guardedness on the outside that gave way to a man who cared hard for the people he loved; the very competent, ever-professional surgeon who turned out to be humble and down-to-earth on the inside.

Mariah had dated lookers before — God knew as a self-proclaimed flirt she'd pretty much dated every type of guy — but after a handful of drop-dead beautiful men, she'd tended to steer clear of them because they were mostly shallow and self-centered, some of them, more than other types, with an unbearable side serving of asshole. Though good looks were nice to gaze at and be seen with, at age twenty-nine, she was more concerned about the soul behind the exterior.

Sawyer had a beautiful soul. One that spoke to her, in spite of the potentially embarrassing, fully innocent night they'd spent together. That they'd slept in the same bed all night and hadn't so much as kissed … for some reason, she found that kind of endearing. A tiny bit disappointing, yes, but truthfully, she'd been too tipsy last night to properly appreciate sex with Sawyer Culver. When it happened — and it would if she had her way — she wanted to be fully alert and able to savor every second of it, every inch of him.

When he'd disappeared to the bathroom as she'd made a second pot of coffee — shortly after midnight, she remembered — she'd been perplexed at first when he hadn't come back. The sight that had met her when she'd gone looking for him, however, was still burned into her mind's eye, and if she had any say in it, it always would be. Sawyer, who'd drunk a lot more than her, thanks to her brother's rowdy firefighter friends and the nature of the male ego, had apparently stripped his clothes off and climbed into her bed. She'd found him stretched out on his stomach on top of the unmade bed, his perfect ass in plain, heart-stopping view. His face had been toward her, his tanned arms extended above his head to grasp her pillow, a position that did incredible justice to the muscles in his back and arms.

He was a brainiac doctor, but he apparently still found plenty of time to work those biceps.

With her body warm and wanting at the thought, Mariah whipped to her back, eyes open, hoping…

Still no Sawyer.

She pressed her lips together in disappointment and tried to ignore the rush of her pulse.

So he was having doubts. Or feeling embarrassed. Both?

Not good. Not promising at all, but Mariah could work around that. Until Sawyer, she hadn't ever met a man who caused the incessant hum deep inside of her that made her imagine her own white gown and veil. She wasn't going to allow the one who did to get away without at least a first date.

With a strong enough sense of purpose that she could ignore her dull headache, she popped out of bed, started the shower, and began plotting.

THE LAST SAWYER KNEW, salsa dancing did *not* involve a stripper pole.

Shit, not only had he had an ill-advised drunken sleepover but it turned out it'd been with a woman who had moves that should be illegal. He was trying his damnedest to push his life in a new, better, more "grown-up" direction, but it seemed he'd regressed about fifteen years in the past week.

The moves Mariah was making as her body worked its way up the thin pole… Sawyer couldn't peel his eyes from her. She twirled her graceful body, effortlessly grasping the metal with deceptively powerful thighs. As she spun and twisted, her ginger-colored hair flew in a tantalizing circle, making his fingers itch to touch it.

He still had no recollection of touching it — or her — the other night. And at this particular moment, with her alluring body moving like that before his eyes, that became a major regret. Mariah was the sexiest, most alluring woman he'd laid eyes on in some time.

Never mind that she was wearing a utilitarian bodysuit,

performing in an unromantic, fluorescently lit dance studio with four women of various fitness stages looking on. Sawyer was mesmerized. Captivated as she managed some kind of complex vertical spin, writhed down the pole, disengaged herself from it, and ended on her knees with her back arched and her head extended back. He couldn't avert his attention from her slender, exposed neck. Had he tasted that neck?

In an instant, Mariah broke the pose and the spell and popped to her feet with a nod to the other women — pole-dancing students, it appeared. Sawyer was still transfixed, so he saw very clearly the second she spotted him standing there in the front entry room of the dance studio, gawking at her like a love-starved bachelor through the interior window. Her eyes widened momentarily, and then she sent him a private, sultry look that was gone before he could be sure he'd seen it. He frowned, perplexed, and she continued to speak to her students with words he couldn't quite make out as she used her hands to emphasize her message.

Sawyer swallowed hard and looked away, realizing it was a mistake to come here. He should've waited until she was at her apartment. The last thing he needed was images of her twisting that body around a suggestive pole — she'd been in his mind throughout his disastrous day of golf Sunday, as well as at work the past two days, as it was. On the course, he'd held the bottom spot in their foursome, and he hadn't determined which had been more to blame — the hangover or the woman who wouldn't get out of his thoughts. At work, one of the nurses had accused him of being preoccupied more than once, and then she'd made a game out of it. He'd never admit he'd still been puzzling over his weekend.

Call him crazy, but that was not the type of guy he'd hire for the director of surgery if it were his decision. Just because Tennyson wasn't there to witness the debacle he'd made of his life in the past three days, that didn't mean it was okay.

If Mariah hadn't seen him staring at her, he'd get the hell out of here stat. But he'd already wimped out of facing her once.

Time to apologize and get out of her life for good. Focus on the job he still hoped like hell to get.

He moved to the far wall, away from the window, to wait for her class to end — and to fight the urge to get another eyeful of the intriguing, pole-dancing Mariah.

Mariah was off her game big-time.

She'd blown one of the moves she'd been trying to show the class, for starters. Her leg had nearly slipped as she'd demonstrated the brass monkey. Then she'd misread the clock and tried to dismiss them ten minutes early. And now, as her overzealous student, Karen, was going on and on after class about a routine she'd been practicing at home, Mariah realized she'd missed half of what had been said.

All because of the man standing out in the entryway.

At least she hoped Sawyer was still there. Without even considering how the gesture would come across to Karen, Mariah checked the clock again. Shockingly, only two minutes had passed since the other students had left the floor.

"Why don't you show up ten minutes early next week and you can show me," Mariah finally said. "I'd love to see it." She forced enthusiasm into her voice — not something she usually had to do, but if Sawyer left before she got out there … well, she'd just have to chase after him. Because she was not going to miss a chance to talk to him. He'd barely left her mind the past three days.

She pulled on shorts and a tank top over her bodysuit and slid her feet into flip-flops as she bade her last student good-bye. Then she forced herself not to rush to the outer foyer.

God, he was still breathtaking.

"I suspect you gave my ladies a thrill," she said to his profile as he gazed out the front window toward the street. Her voice came out shaky, and she crossed her fingers he didn't notice — or at least didn't realize he was the cause of it. "We don't get eye candy here in the studio very often."

Sawyer pivoted toward her. "I had no idea that's the kind of classes you teach."

He didn't sound judgmental, exactly, just … unsure. Mariah held in a laugh. "Pole-dancing? Every Tuesday night and Sunday afternoon. Sunday's a bigger class, and that's where my professionals are. Tonight's group is more for fitness."

Sawyer looked over his shoulder, out the exterior window, as if he was afraid to be caught here. "Pole-dancing for fitness."

"It takes considerable muscle strength."

"Without a doubt."

"How'd you know where to find me?"

"I was knocking on your door. One of your neighbors set me straight. Short brunette with curly hair?"

"Yasmine." Not usually one who would give out too much of Mariah's information, but she could just imagine her friend's explanation — *When a man like that is looking for your friend, you help him any way possible!*

The door to the locker room opened, and Karen came out with a large gym bag slung over her shoulder. "Dr. Culver, I didn't realize that was you."

Sawyer whipped his head toward her. "Hi, Karen. How are you doing?"

"Doing super. Thanks, in part, to you."

"You look healthy," he said, taking on a professional air, probably without even realizing he did it.

"Gall bladders are overrated anyway," Karen said with a grin. "Do you, um…" Her features twisted in confusion. "Do you dance?"

"No." Sawyer shot a regretful look to Mariah. "I mean, no … not this kind of dancing. Only amateur attempts at weddings…"

He closed his eyes as if also sorry he'd brought up last weekend, and Mariah did laugh.

"He's not half-bad, either," she said. "Didn't step on my toes once."

"Oh." Karen's expression morphed to understanding. "*Oh.* You two—"

"My brother married his sister last weekend," Mariah explained, considering herself extra merciful tonight. Though Sawyer's discomfort was kind of cute, she had no desire to mess with his professionalism.

"Amazing! Oh, there's my ride. Good to see you, Dr. Culver. Night, Mariah."

And they were left alone. Just the way Mariah wanted it. Next challenge, keeping him close for more than two minutes.

"I'm heading to the juice bar down the block. Want to come with?" she asked.

"Juice bar… I guess I could do that."

"Let me grab my bag." Mariah hurried into the locker room and got her stuff, worried Sawyer would bolt again. When she came back out thirty seconds later, she got the full-on light, bubbly sensation in her chest and heard the *yesss* in her mind again just from looking at him. "You're still here," she said lightly.

"Did you think I would— Ah." Sawyer sported a self-effacing grin. "Guess I do have a history of deserting you, don't I?"

They went to the door, and Mariah slipped beneath his arm out into the balmy May evening as he held it open for her.

SAWYER CAUGHT a hint of her scent as she passed. It was exotic and feminine, with an earthy undertone from the workout she'd just finished.

"It was no big deal," she said as she locked up. "I remembered you had to golf."

Sawyer didn't remember telling her he had to golf, of course.

"Tee time or not, I should have told you I was leaving. I … I flipped out a little. Not my standard MO, actually."

"Flipping out?" He felt Mariah studying him from the side as they walked along the sidewalk. "I can kind of see that's not your norm. You seem … pretty cool in general."

If only she knew how uncool she makes me…

"Cool is not a word I would use for the way I acted Saturday night. And I was referring to shacking up for a night with a woman I barely know. I'm sorry, Mariah. That was not me."

"Weddings are crazy. Always. I don't know what it is that makes the guests go so nuts — other than free alcohol, of course."

"My head hurt for two full days."

She laughed, a sexy, musical sound that drew him in in spite of himself. "I was worried about you."

"I was fine. By morning anyway. There was nothing fine about me the night of the wedding. I should never have gone to your place."

"No worries. I invited you. Seems like a good thing you didn't try to walk the rest of the way home."

It was probably true, and wasn't that admirable too? Sawyer's embarrassment flared.

"I'm never drinking tequila again," he said. "I'm old enough to know better and then some."

"So you said Saturday night," Mariah said lightly. "About thirty times."

He shook his head.

"Hey," she said, and she startled him by hooking her arm through his. "Don't be so hard on yourself. We drank too much. We had fun. No one got hurt. It's all good."

He wished he could take it so lightly. She made it tempting to figure out how to let it go.

Mariah didn't immediately release her arm, and though he shouldn't, Sawyer savored her touch. Just for a couple of minutes, he told himself.

The silence stretched on as they walked the last block, and he became aware of how close they were and how bad of an idea that was. He slowed and took his cell phone out of his pocket. As he'd hoped, she put space between them and let go of his arm.

"Thought I had a text," he said. "I might have to go check on a patient yet tonight."

Which wasn't entirely true. Yeah, he was throwing up roadblocks. Being with her made his poor judgment, his regret impossible to ignore. A lot of guys wouldn't think twice about being an idiot for a night, but he wasn't a lot of guys.

He was supposed to be upping his life game. Getting his shit together. His general surgery position was decent, but he was from a family of overachievers, and even his little sister was primed to leave him in the dust. His mom had gone out on a limb to give him an in, a connection that could help land him a better job with more responsibility. He was past the point of wild partying and impetuous decisions. In theory.

The plan was to handle his fuck-up like a man, apologize to Mariah, and get on with his life, but he found it hard to say no to this redhead.

4

They arrived at the juice bar. Sawyer opened the door for Mariah and avoided catching her scent as she passed so closely.

"What's good?" he asked her as she went straight to the clerk at the counter with no hesitation about her order.

"Almost everything. I'm getting the Triple Berry Crush."

"Make it two."

"I know you," the scrawny teenaged boy behind the counter said to Sawyer. "You're my mom's surgeon."

Sawyer scanned his memory to match the face with a patient. "Beverly Adams is your mom, right?"

"Yeah." The kid grinned. "She sings your praises to all her friends, man. She's like a new person. Like an alien took over her body or something. In a good way, I mean."

"As long as it's a good way," Sawyer said with a smile. Procedures like the one Bev Adams had tended to give people a new attitude, he found.

"So two Triple Berry Crushes, right?"

"Thanks, Tanner," Mariah, obviously a regular, said.

Sawyer was watching the boy prepare their concoctions, mildly curious what he'd ordered, when he realized Mariah was eyeing him from the side. He silently questioned her with a dip of his brows. She shrugged and smiled, ignoring his query and getting them both straws from the dispenser.

As Tanner finished up their drinks on the blender, Sawyer pulled out his wallet. He wasn't able to date this woman, but he sure as hell wasn't going to make her pay for his drink.

"Thank you," Mariah said as they turned away from the counter. "Next one's on me."

And … he needed to clear up the misconception that there'd be a next one. "Mariah…"

"Want to drink here or take them with us?"

Sawyer glanced at his watch and swore to himself. He'd planned to go to the chamber of commerce ribbon-cutting ceremony for the new surgical wing at St. Mary's Regional, where he'd interviewed. Dr. Tennyson would undoubtedly be there, and not only would it score points and hopefully boost his chances at the job offer by being seen, but if he did get that position, this new wing would be a big part of his future. Going was a no-brainer.

The ceremony started in … five minutes. It was a fifteen-minute drive from his car to the hospital if he hit all the lights right. Once again, he'd gotten carried away with this woman, this time watching her dance.

"What's wrong?" Mariah asked, her hand on one of the chairs at a table by the window. She looked up at him with green eyes that were naturally sultry. "You don't like the Triple Berry?"

It took him a second to realize he hadn't even tried the concoction yet. His mind spinning in a handful of directions, he raised the straw to his lips and sipped. The sweet, creamy, berry flavor seduced his tongue — or maybe that was the woman standing inches away from him. The woman he didn't want to leave just yet. "It's really good. Potentially addictive."

"Tell me about it. I get one every day I work. So…?" Her eyes questioned him again.

Screw the ribbon cutting. Either he'd nailed the interview and was the best candidate for the job … or not. Showing up for some face time with Dr. Tennyson wasn't going to change the outcome.

The chief of surgery didn't know Sawyer had planned to show up, so he wouldn't know the difference when Sawyer skipped it.

He could allow himself a few extra minutes with this bewitching woman. And then, when he walked away, he'd walk away for good. One evening, just a few minutes, would not change the direction of his future.

"Let's walk over to the fountain on the square," he suggested, not wanting to hurry their time together and unwilling to have Tanner listen in on their conversation. They said good-bye to the clerk and went back out into the humid Texas night.

"Does everybody on the island know you?" Mariah asked once they'd started walking.

Sawyer chuckled. "Hardly."

"We've been together for about ten minutes now, and we're two for two."

"Weird night, I guess." Weird week.

"I think it's cool. You're, I don't know, this big-time important guy in the community. Looked up to. Almost like a mini-celebrity. Can't even get a juice without your public finding you." Her voice had become louder and animated as she poured it on.

"It's a tough existence," he said, smiling. "If they'd just let me drink in peace."

She laughed and the sound touched something inside of him again.

Sawyer cleared his throat. "I'll actually miss that a little if I get the job I interviewed for. Running in to patients. Being able to see how they're doing."

"The job. Director of surgery at St. Mary's, right?"

He whipped his head toward her. "How'd—"

"You told me all about it Saturday night. Apparently during the part of the night you don't remember." There was no derision in her voice, only lightness and good nature.

That didn't make him feel any better.

"There are parts of the … conversation that night that are a little hazy."

Hello, understatement. He still hadn't gotten back a ten-hour chunk or so. That he'd been passed out for part of that — without his clothes — was not reassuring.

"As first dates go, it wasn't my finest hour either," Mariah said. "So I was thinking maybe we need a do-over."

"I…" He couldn't. Regardless of how much he liked the flirty arch of her brow as she matched his pace with her long legs. When you got down to it, he could barely look at her without feeling like a guilt-ridden teenager. Starting anything intentionally with Mariah would be pointless.

"Not an exact do-over. No fancy clothes, no wedding insanity, no tequila."

They reached the square, a courtyard in the middle of a shopping district with a dolphin fountain as the centerpiece and various flowering bushes and perennials scattered among quaint, wrought-iron benches. Without discussing it, they sat on one of the benches facing the fountain.

It was time to level with her. He'd indulged himself by bringing her to the square, spending more time with her, but he had to stop. "I don't think that's a good idea," he forced out.

Mariah's head tilted. "The no fancy clothes? Or the do-over? Maybe do-over isn't a good word for it. I just meant—"

"I can't go out with you, Mariah. Fancy or no. It's… We wound up together during an ill-advised night. Like I told you, that wasn't me at all."

"I'd like to get to know the real you," she said boldly, pegging him with those eyes again.

"The real me doesn't have time right now to devote to … a woman like you." A woman who could turn him into a man who made irresponsible decisions. A woman who could make him lose sight of his priorities.

"A woman like me?"

A-back-pedaling we will go…

"You deserve someone who can give you all his focus. I … can't." Which was true, even if he was laying it on thick. "I shouldn't even be here right now. I'm supposed to be at a ribbon-cutting ceremony kissing up to Dr. Ramon Tennyson, Chief of Surgery."

"The guy you interviewed with."

"One of them, yes…"

"You played golf with him Sunday."

"Is there anything I didn't tell you Saturday night?" he said, attempting to keep his laugh light and not self-conscious.

"We talked for a long time — I think." Mariah grinned shyly. "It's not the clearest night in my memory either. If I did something or said something to offend you, I'm sorry."

"Not at all," he answered quickly. "The opposite, really. It's the way I acted that's offensive. Which is why I tracked you down tonight."

She turned her body toward him on the bench, hooking her arm over the back and bringing them closer together. "You've already apologized, Sawyer." His elbows were propped on his knees, and Mariah ran her finger absently down his forearm and back up. Her touch did way more to him than such a light, insignificant touch should do. Then her head snapped up as if she realized what she was doing. "It's okay. We're cool. And we should probably get back to the studio. Maybe you can still make it to the ribbon cutting."

He took a final drink of Triple Berry and tossed the mostly empty cup into the trash can a couple of feet away. "It'd be too late by the time I got there, but yeah, we should get back." Regret at his decision to skip the event was already building in his chest. He stood abruptly, and Mariah rose as well.

Without meaning to, he faced her at the exact moment she faced him. Their gazes locked, her green eyes intensely focused on his, and he felt something in his chest dip. Fall. His eyes followed suit, without his permission, and lowered to her lips. Her soft, moist, tempting lips that were parted slightly in invitation. He looked back at her eyes in time to see them lower to his mouth, and that small action was enough to set off an alarm in his head. If he kissed her, walking away would be harder. It was better that he didn't remember how she kissed, because he had an overwhelming suspicion that Mariah's kisses would be magical.

Sawyer forced his eyes away and his mind to the regret still simmering just below the surface, and as he knew would happen, the trance was broken. He swallowed, took a step back, and said, "Ready?"

The point he privately scored for resisting his urge to taste those sensual lips paled as the larger picture sank in. Skipping the ceremony tonight was yet another poor, impulsive decision. Once again, he'd veered straight off the path he was trying like hell to stay on. And once again, this woman was at the heart of his foolishness.

5

―――――――

One last chance.

Mariah was giving herself one last opportunity to see Sawyer. And okay, she was giving Sawyer a final chance to give in to what she could swear was some serious chemistry between them. Chemistry and beyond.

He'd rejected her the other night after the juice shop, but his excuse was lame. Didn't have time to date? She could accept that he was super busy. She respected that the prospect of a new job would take his focus away from his personal life for a while. But not once had he said he didn't like her, and in fact, his body language said he did.

So she was going to test her theory.

Today — Friday — was his day off if she remembered right. Though she'd never been to his apartment, she knew where it was — yet another advantage of his chattiness last Saturday night. It took a considerable self-pep talk to get herself out the door, but once she was in her car, she was consumed by the mission. Determined to give it her all, because there was too much at stake to let this — whatever *this* was between them — go without her best effort. Not when just being near him set off alarms in her head and gave her romantic notions she'd never entertained before.

One kiss. That was the lump sum of her plan. One kiss, and either she'd know her reaction to him was all in her head or…

Or they'd both know it wasn't.

Kisses didn't lie.

IT WAS FRIDAY. Day of reckoning. Sawyer glared at the half-eaten apple he'd forced himself to get for lunch, then tossed it in the kitchen wastebasket.

You'll hear something by the end of next week, they'd said during the full day of interviews.

It was as end-of-next-week as you could get. Though he might still get a phone call, it wouldn't be a good one. They'd call the person they wanted to hire first — probably already had a couple days ago — and then they'd eventually get around to notifying the losers.

Though he'd held out his hopes before today, now it was undeniable — things did not look good.

He checked his email on his phone for the four hundredth time in case they didn't have the balls to give him the bad news with a phone call, but there was no message.

Sawyer slid his phone across the kitchen counter with more than a little force and strode angrily from the room, swearing at himself the whole way. He ended up in front of the living room window, staring out at the appropriately stormy day, watching the palm trees three levels down bend in the wind.

He'd screwed up. Repeatedly.

He'd thought the interviews went well, but who ever knew? He'd been dumb enough to believe that having his mom's connection with Ramon Tennyson would boost his chances, but he knew better. It might have gotten him the interview, but it sure as hell hadn't gotten him the job. Then he'd sealed his fate by showing up for his tee time with Tennyson with only twenty-five percent of his brain cells firing. He could have possibly smoothed over that stupidity by being on his game Wednesday for the ribbon cutting, but no. He'd fucked that up too.

The peal of the doorbell startled him out of his pity party. Who the hell…? He wasn't in the mood to see anyone.

He ignored the first two rings, and then he crept to the peephole. Tall woman. Red hair.

What was Mariah doing here? He opened the door without further deliberation, and as he looked at her in full view, standing a foot in front of him, there was an instant when he felt … relief? A moment of comfort during his internal tsunami. He ignored that strange thought and drank in the sight of her instead. What guy wouldn't? Her auburn hair fell smoothly down her back with a few stray strands slipping over her shoulders, drawing his attention to her breasts. She was dressed in her unique, attention-grabbing way, wearing a gauzy, translucent blouse over a delicate camisole that exposed cleavage. A modest amount, but it had his mouth going dry nonetheless. Her shorts … her legs … shit. She was exactly the type of long-legged woman clothes designers created *short*-shorts for. Short-shorts like the ones she was wearing. Those legs were made for…

"Hey, Sawyer. I was about to leave. Glad I didn't." The tilt of her head was friendly and open, and yet he saw all kinds of sexual undertones in it. Probably unintentional on her part. Everything about Mariah oozed sexuality. She could gasp for breath after a run on the beach and he'd be turned on.

Her smile faded. "Is something wrong?"

Sawyer blinked hard and chased his inappropriate thoughts away. "No. Come on in." He opened the door wider for her and wondered at the same time if that was ill-advised. No. He wanted to see Mariah right now. Needed the refuge she offered from his state of mind. If there was anything that could keep him from losing his shit over the lack of a phone call, this beautiful redhead was it.

"I remembered you said you didn't have to work today," she said as she walked past him toward the living room.

Sawyer couldn't help it — he checked out her ass in those shorts and got lost in the fantasy of touching her where the white material ended.

"You remember a lot," he said distractedly.

"Only the important stuff. You really do seem down," she said as she set her purse on the coffee table. "Is everything okay?"

He exhaled and closed his eyes briefly, all his worry collapsing back around him after a two-minute break brought on by lustful thoughts. "I didn't get the job."

"What?" She stepped toward him, her brows furrowed in disbelief. "Are you kidding me?"

He shook his head.

"No. Of course you're not," she said as if to herself. "What the hell? Why wouldn't they choose you, Sawyer? You're good at your job, amazing—"

"Someone is obviously better."

"When did you find out?"

He looked away and walked to the glass door to the balcony. "They haven't called yet, but if they were going to hire me, I'd know." The wind outside gusted suddenly, blowing the folding chair on the balcony into the adobe wall.

Mariah came up behind him. "Then you don't actually know for sure. You're assuming?"

He watched the trees bend below for a beat before answering. "Yes, if you want to get technical."

She touched his shoulder blade, and he felt his blood warm. Sawyer turned to her.

"It's" — she checked the delicate silver watch around her slender wrist, then rested her hand on his chest — "just after two o'clock. You have no idea what's going on in their offices or their lives. You never know until you hear for sure."

The inside of her wrist was delicate-looking and much better to think about than the non-phone call.

"You know I'm right," Mariah said.

He dragged his gaze from her arm to her eyes.

"You know *I'm* right that they would've called by now if it was a yes. Quit trying to make me feel better long enough to admit the truth."

Mariah seemed to debate with herself for several seconds

before shrugging. "They should have. I hate when people don't do what they say they will. It sucks to be left hanging."

Defeat pulsed in his throat. He blew out a heavy breath and knocked the back of his head into the window. "It's okay. I'm not even sure how much I wanted it..."

Mariah nodded knowingly. "It's less time with patients. More bureaucracy."

He froze at the bull's-eye she'd just hit with her words, then scowled.

"You explained it Saturday night," she said.

"Of course I did." *Fuck.* Saturday night was going to kill him yet.

"You said it'd be a lot of administration *crap*, I believe was your word."

"I like what I do now. Patient care is the whole reason I went into medicine. So the real question is why the hell I applied for the job in the first place."

"Pressure. Your family."

Saturday goddamn night, he thought as he strived to keep his expression from giving away how much he didn't remember. He shook his head and stalked away from the window toward the open kitchen. "I guess." He opened his fridge and took out a bottle of beer. "Want a drink?"

"I'm good," she said. "Your mom and sister are overachievers, you told me."

Sawyer popped off the lid and took a long drink. He set the bottle down hard on the breakfast bar that separated the kitchen space from the living room. "Always have been."

"You said you feel pressure to do more. That being a general surgeon isn't enough. You sometimes wish you'd gone on to specialize, but since you didn't, you think you should take on more responsibility."

The truth in her words was as disconcerting as not remembering the conversation at all.

Sawyer considered himself an optimist and sort of bought into the whole "focusing on the good in everything" philosophy. What Mariah was saying — which was obviously what had come out of his mouth originally — was negative. Doubtful. And okay, he could acknowledge it, fear-based. He wanted to deny it all and tell her it'd been tequila-induced nonsense, but he couldn't quite convince himself.

"My mom introduced me to Ramon Tennyson. That's not an opportunity I could afford to blow." Just thinking about facing up to her, admitting to her he'd failed…

Once again, he found himself at the glass door, gazing out as if there were a solution out there. Fat raindrops began to pelt the outer edge of the covered balcony.

"Hey," Mariah said, coming up behind him again and standing close enough he could feel her heat.

It would've been wiser for him to stay in the kitchen with the bar separating them. Without his permission, his body turned around to face her.

"Things happen for a reason," she said. "That might be a cliché, but I believe it. *If* you don't get this job, then it wasn't the right thing. However, there's several hours left in the week, Dr. Pessimist. A lot can happen in an hour or two." Her gaze lowered toward his mouth for a moment.

"Yeah?" he said, suddenly having a hard time speaking. His back was against the glass pane, and she pressed her body along the front of his.

"Absolutely."

Mariah lifted her chin and kissed him.

6

Mariah's lips brushed Sawyer's with a whisper of a touch at first. Testing. Teasing.

Sawyer instinctively grasped her waist in both hands. Pulled her into him. Leaned in for more. The second meeting of their lips was firm. Urgent. Hot as hell. It took less than a heartbeat for his cock to go hard and his blood to boil.

Mariah moaned, and he tilted his head for better access, his tongue exploring her lips, her mouth, darting into her heat, making him think about other moist, hot places on her body.

A part of him knew this went against his plan, but at the moment, his plan was out the window. Kissing Mariah felt like the only thing that made sense. There was refuge in her touch. Respite from his disappointment. How could he worry about *anything* with her in his arms?

He burned with the need to touch her, to know her in ways others didn't. Their hands were everywhere, on top of clothing, slipping beneath, caressing, burning. God, she was hot. Passionate. She made him forget everything except the heat between them that was building to explosive levels in record time.

They were both breathing hard when Mariah broke the contact of their lips and pulled her head back. Alarmed, he opened his eyes to see what was wrong and was relieved to see her smile with a seductiveness he was beginning to expect from her.

"Exactly what I thought," she said, her voice thick with desire.

Then her hands trailed back up his chest, to the back of his neck, and their tongues met again, meshed and tangled and… Sawyer forgot his curiosity at her words.

Seconds later, she had his shirt off and dropped it to the floor. Her aggressiveness turned him on even more, and he craved her skin. Bare, silky flesh. And those legs…

Sawyer grasped the backs of her thighs right below her ass and edged his fingers up beneath her shorts. Softness and heat. He needed more, needed her closer. Lifting her, he turned their bodies until Mariah's back was pressed against the glass. She wrapped her legs around him, nestling him at her core and pulling a growl from deep in Sawyer's throat.

Within seconds, he had her down to a lacy lavender bra and barely there panties. Her fingers dipped into his shorts, first in back, then at his fly. He felt his snap give, heard his zipper go down. Then she grazed his tip and … *holy hell.*

"Mariah," he managed. "We're treading close to that point…" A full stroke from her had his words and thoughts stopping abruptly and his brain melting.

"Are you not okay with this?" she whispered. "We can stop…"

Stopping, not getting to drive her body to oblivion the way she was doing with him, was not an option. To hell with the job, the plan, everything. It wasn't like this was new ground, exactly — just new to his memory. He wanted this with her, wanted to remember what it felt like to be wrapped in Mariah's long, beautiful thighs. So he was being impulsive … again. So fucking what?

"More than okay," he forced out. "But if you don't stop *that,* it's going to be over quicker than either of us want."

"Yeah?" she said with a grin that was both smug and sultry at once. She stroked him again, once, twice, and every drop of blood swarmed south, every nerve in his body tuned in to her touch.

The best defense is a good offense.

Sawyer reached between them and pulled her hand from his pants, twisting their fingers together as he braced her body more securely between his and the glass. He held her hand above her head and trailed his other to her breast, pushing the thin material of her bra down so he had full access to her nipple. She arched into him and threw her head back as he teased one side with his thumb and finger, his palm, then moved to the other side.

MARIAH HEARD the needy sounds she made, but she didn't care. She just … wanted. *More.* Wanted him to relieve the ache that throbbed at her center, intensifying with every second of contact. She was only remotely aware that he had her up against the door where, technically, the world could see them.

Determined to get to him, she dropped her hands back to his waist and under his shorts to knead his ass. As he teased her with his tongue, she eased his shorts and boxer briefs down and pushed them to the floor, leaving him beautifully naked. Of course, she couldn't see how beautifully just now because he was still making her crazy with his fingers and tongue and… *Oh, God.*

"Sawyer," she moaned as she rubbed her body against his heat. Her breathing went shallow as she felt the velvet touch of him on her inner thigh at the edge of her underwear.

"Hold on," he said, and as he moved them away from the window, she threw her arms around his neck even though he had a solid grasp of her butt.

"What are you doing?" she asked as he carried her through the living room.

"No one needs to see us." He took her into his bedroom and eased her onto the center of his bed on top of the covers.

"You have to admit it was kind of hot."

"You're naughtier than you look," he said with an appreciative look. "I strongly believe that public sex should only happen when two people are, you know, seriously dating, at the very least."

"I do adore a guy with morals."

His modesty was sweet, and if she were thinking straight, she'd no doubt be appreciative of his control, as well. While sex against the sliding glass door might be incredibly stimulating at the time, she would probably die of embarrassment as soon as the moment was over. *Walk of shame* would take on new meaning.

"Come here," she whispered. She pulled him down closer and kissed him again as she wrapped her legs around him.

"Don't have to tell me twice."

His body pressed at her opening, her underwear and bra the only things keeping them apart. As if he read her thoughts, he reached behind her back and fumbled around for a couple of seconds before unclasping her bra. He whisked it off her and palmed both her breasts, caressing and stroking them reverently.

Now Mariah could fully admire his beauty. Doctors were not supposed to look like that, she thought distractedly, her breath coming irregularly. She writhed against him, edgy, dying for him to fill her, to ease the burning need.

"Sawyer."

He moved his body enough to peel her underwear down her legs. Mariah lifted her knees and arched needily.

"Do you have something?" he breathed into her ear. His tongue toyed with her lobe and his tip teased her core, making it hard as hell to register the question.

"It's taken care of," she said. Between timing and the pill, she wouldn't be getting pregnant today.

"If you're sure," Sawyer said, and he entered her, easing himself in inch by incredible inch, taking it slowly enough for her body to stretch and accommodate him. Mariah sank her teeth into his shoulder and let herself be carried away as her body adjusted and he moved inside of her.

Her thoughts stopped, and all she knew was the over-whelming sensation of Sawyer everywhere. Inside her and outside. The scent of the two of them together, the sounds of their bodies moving as one, the weight of him on top of her, the surprisingly graphic things he whispered into her ear, the touch of his fingers, on her nipples, her skin, at the apex of her legs. It was too much, too much … and yet not enough. She was climbing, reaching, making more noise than she'd normally be comfortable with but, oh, my god, how could she not? And then her whole body was tingling and burning and tensing and bursting.

Mariah arched and held her body against Sawyer's as he continued to thrust into her, saying her name, making the sexiest sounds, sweating, stiffening with his own climax.

He held her to him as he rolled to his side, breathing hard, a grin overtaking his beautiful face, softening the hard angles and sending a shiver of the best kind through Mariah. She tucked her head into his chest and curled into him just as a crack of thunder rent into the afternoon storm, making her jump and then laugh.

"How appropriate," Sawyer said in a husky, sated voice. "Sums up the experience pretty damn well."

"I think that's a good sign," Mariah said with a questioning tone.

"Good is a mild word for it."

"For me too."

Their bodies were damp with a sheen of sweat, and the breeze that came in the open window was suddenly chilly. Sawyer pulled the blankets out from under them and drew the sheet over them.

"You have to tell me … what did you mean when you said 'exactly as I thought'?" he asked.

"What? When?"

"When you kissed me. That's what you said."

"Ah, yes." Mariah laughed lazily, feeling so damn content. "If I tell you, you can't get mad."

Sawyer grinned. "It'd take an epic something to get me mad right now."

"Well, you see, there was sort of this test."

"What kind of test?"

"Kissing you."

"That was a *test*? Did I pass?"

"We passed."

"What did we pass?"

She trailed her finger around on his chest, up the ridges and down the dip between his pecs.

"You were giving me mixed signals," she said. "Before today, I mean. So I decided a kiss wouldn't lie."

He frowned. "About?"

"Whether there was something between us. A spark, I guess. We've slept in the same bed, and we've come close to kissing, or at least I thought we had, but then I thought maybe I'd imagined it, you know? So I decided to just go for it and find out, once and for all."

Sawyer had been twirling his finger in a lock of her hair, but he stopped the movement cold.

Come close to kissing? That was all?

He'd gone out of his way to apologize to her on Wednesday… for nothing? He'd beat himself up all week, not for nothing, because the mere fact that he didn't know what had happened or not happened warranted a large amount of self-disgust, but the one-night-stand element was high on the list of reasons to regret last weekend. The *nonexistent* one-night stand.

"What's wrong, Sawyer? You don't agree that we passed?"

He briefly registered the alarm in Mariah's eyes, but that was nothing compared to his panic in the next second.

7

The knock at the front door carried in through the open bedroom door. The frantic, insistent knock.

"Sawyer! Open up!"

"Oh, my god!" Mariah hopped out of bed. "Is that your mom?"

Sawyer was about point-two seconds behind her, rushing around the room in search of their clothing.

"Your clothes are in the living room," he said.

Mariah was in the next room before his words were all the way out, and then she was darting into his bathroom and slamming the door. Sawyer pulled on the first clothing items he found — a pair of dirty jeans from the floor and a T-shirt from the top of the clean laundry pile. Underwear at this point was unnecessary. Déjà vu.

"You about done?" he said in a low voice through the bathroom door.

"Getting there."

"Sawyer! I know you're home! I saw your car!" His mom attempted to beat down the door.

"Stay in the bathroom," he told Mariah. "I'll get rid of her. Coming," he said more loudly as he headed to the front door.

He opened it with his eyebrows raised. "Is your phone broken?"

"Is yours?" Jackie Culver rushed past him. "Ramon Tennyson has been trying to call you for the past hour plus, Sawyer. It doesn't look good that he can't get ahold of you to offer you a job."

"He didn't offer me a job." Sawyer was caught between trying to make sense of what his mom said, making sure Mariah stayed put in the bathroom, and coming up with an explanation if she did come out.

"He's trying to! Where's your phone?"

His mom's words sank in, and he looked around for the phone. He rushed into the kitchen and picked it up off the counter. The screen was blank. "Battery must have died. Are you sure he plans to make an offer? I gave up when he hadn't called by noon."

"His daughter-in-law has been in the hospital all week. I ran into him in the hall when he was visiting her this afternoon, and he mentioned he'd been trying to call you. I knew you didn't work today, so I was a little concerned."

"I might've been taking a nap, you know," he said, purposely misleading her.

"You always answer the phone when you're not on duty."

"Except when my battery's dead." He opened a kitchen drawer and pulled out a phone charger, then plugged it in. It took several seconds for the phone to register that it had juice from the outlet.

"There. It's plugged in. I'll call him in five minutes, as soon as I have a little charge," he told his mom.

"I'll wait." She was all grins, proud as punch that her slacker son was finally about to go places.

"Really, Mom. Some privacy?"

She managed to look crestfallen, which jabbed at his conscience more than a little.

"Please," he said. "I'll call you as soon as I have details. I'll take you to dinner to celebrate sometime."

His mom laughed giddily, as if she were the one getting a job offer. Sawyer wondered briefly why he didn't share the elation.

Must be that the news hadn't sunk in yet. Or that he was too preoccupied by the woman hiding out in his bathroom.

"That's fine," his mother said. "You're right. This is your moment, and you can handle it the way you want. I'll leave you in peace."

"Thanks." He led her toward the door, shoulders relaxing slightly, but he wouldn't let his guard down all the way until she was gone and Mariah was undiscovered. The last thing he needed was for his mom to discover he'd had an afternoon screw with a girl he barely knew. Even if she was almost family.

"If I don't hear from you within thirty minutes, I'll hunt you down," his mom said in a falsely threatening voice. "Understand?"

"You'll hear." He opened the door for her. "Thanks for the heads-up. Good-bye, Mom."

She stared at him for a lingering moment, beaming. "Go make your call."

He shut the door behind her and leaned on it, eyes closed. He'd barely let loose of his breath when he heard his phone ring.

MARIAH OPENED the bathroom door cautiously at first. She wasn't wild about the idea of Sawyer's mom figuring out why she was here, but she and Sawyer were adults. They didn't have to explain themselves to anyone.

"Yes, sir," she heard Sawyer say in a businesslike voice. Definitely not talking to his mom anymore. She was almost certain she'd heard the female Dr. Culver leave.

She poked her head out, and Sawyer glanced over at her distractedly. Before she could fully emerge, he'd walked into his bedroom and shut the door.

Okay, then.

This wasn't good. He'd been borderline flipping out just before his mom had shown up, and now ... now he didn't so much as smile at her on his way past. Yes, he was busy on the phone, and she understood that, but a little grin would've gone a long way toward reassuring her.

She suspected reassurance wasn't on the top of his mind. Or even in the top ten layers.

She wandered into the living room and discovered the shirt she'd taken off him draped over the lamp at the end of the couch. *Fantastic.* She hoped Dr. Culver had missed that.

As Mariah circled the room aimlessly, she could hear Sawyer's muffled voice in the other room. Very official sounding. A hearty laugh here and there. But she couldn't make out the words. At last, the bedroom door opened, and she heard Sawyer tell his caller good-bye. She waited for him to round the corner.

When he did, he wouldn't meet her eyes. He seemed preoccupied, and she wasn't even sure he knew she was still there.

"Is everything okay?" she asked from her spot by the glass door — the glass door she'd recently been nearly naked against.

"I got the job." And yet he still wasn't looking at her.

"Sawyer! That's spectacular! Congratulations."

He shuffled over to the couch and sat on the arm, a couple feet away from her. "Thanks." His forehead was wrinkled with concern. "Mariah, this afternoon was a mistake."

Disbelief jolted through her. "Really? A mistake?"

"Yes," he said quietly.

"See, I think of a mistake more like when you do a math problem and you accidentally add instead of multiply so you get the wrong answer. Or when you're doing a dance routine and you fall on your ass, and the whole audience knows because there's no way to camouflage it. Not when something happens that's freaking out-of-this-world amazing, that practically alters the tilt of the earth on its axis."

"It shouldn't have happened. It wasn't fair of me to let it happen."

"I don't think you could have stopped it if you'd tried. It happened for a reason, Sawyer."

He chuffed air out, almost like a laugh, but there was no humor in it. "It was a weak moment for both of us. We let our guard down."

"If you have to keep your guard up to keep from having *that* happen, then you might need to rethink your priorities."

"I told you what my priorities are." He stood and strode to the opposite side of the room. After tossing his cell phone on the kitchen bar, he exhaled and faced her — though she noticed he didn't look directly at her. "It has nothing to do with you, Mariah—"

"Awesome," she broke in sarcastically. "One of those 'it's-not-you-it's-me' speeches." She choked out a laugh. "The one guy I could get serious about, and instead I get a cliché."

"Look how we got together. We were too drunk to stand up straight, let alone make a well-thought-out decision. I…" He swallowed and looked at the ceiling. "I didn't know until today that we didn't, in fact, sleep together. *That* is not how you start a promising relationship."

"That was a fluke for both of us, Sawyer. You may think it was just another Saturday night for flirty Mariah, but I don't let just any guy stay at my house. I've never let a man stay in that apartment with me for the four years I've lived there."

His eyes sought out hers, though only for a moment, and then he shook his head shortly, scowling. "I don't think that of you. I don't know you, Mariah. You don't know me. We got together because we were stewed, not because we have hope of making a good couple."

Mariah bolstered herself against the pain of his words and straightened boldly. She wasn't the type to shy away from something she cared about — and, stupidly or not, she cared about Sawyer. "We may have ended up having a slumber party because of the alcohol, but I'm here to tell you, in my experience, what just happened in your bedroom wasn't something that occurs every day. Or every year. Or, I'll go out on a limb and say, every lifetime."

"That was chemistry."

"Yes! A vital part of any good couple." She shook her head. "We're not a couple, no, but … you haven't given us a chance."

Sawyer closed his eyes. "I can't. I'm sorry. With this new job—"

"Stop," Mariah broke in. This was going nowhere good. What had started out as amazing was rapidly getting ruined. There was no way she could change his mind — not if what had happened between them less than an hour ago couldn't do it. She clenched her jaw. Nodded once. "As you mentioned, you told me your priorities the other day. My bad." She picked up her purse off the table and headed toward the door. "Good luck with your amazing new job." She bit her tongue before she could say she hoped it kept him warm at night and walked out of his condo.

Sawyer had issues, obviously, and it was now crystal clear to her that they were more than she could help him through. Which sounded cut-and-dried enough, but it didn't come close to preventing her tears from blinding her on the way to her car.

8

"You might as well level with me, Sawyer. What's wrong with you today?"

He felt that familiar mom stare coming at him, drilling into his face from the side. The one that didn't relent, that didn't let him get by with a "nothing much" reply. He hated the mom stare.

And yet he had no answer for her.

They stood in the airport terminal Sunday afternoon waiting for his sister and her new husband's return from their honeymoon. Several others who'd been part of the small wedding ceremony last week waited with them, though Sawyer and Jackie were off to the side, leaning against a wall, keeping to themselves for now.

Sawyer had been antsy all weekend. Jittery. Bothered. Ever since Friday afternoon. He'd like to be able to attribute it to excitement over the job offer but…

Without realizing it, he shook his head. Blew out his breath. "I don't know, Mom."

Instead of the snappy disagreement he expected, she continued to study him for several seconds, her forehead furrowing. "Hard to tell you just got a fabulous job offered to you."

Sawyer bit down on any defense. He hated this feeling of unease, that his life was "off."

"You're calling Ramon tomorrow to accept?" his mom asked quietly.

Question of the hour.

Movement to their right caught his attention. Not just any movement: approach by a redhead. A drop-dead, knockout, attention-grabbing redhead.

Mariah hurried toward the larger group, her long legs carrying her on graceful strides, hair trailing loosely behind her, reminding him of how it'd looked spread out on his pillow. It took sincere willpower to stay where he was on the wall in an attempt to not come across like an eager puppy. She glanced over and spotted him. Frowned.

He deserved her anger.

Even mad as hell at him, she was alluring. She stood out in any crowd, especially today. She was dressed in a floral bandeau-style top, a flowy, orange skirt that hit her thigh well above her knee, and an intricate bunch of beads and charms that hung from her neck, some of them down to her flat navel. On her feet were strappy heels and nail polish that matched her skirt and made him want a closer look. Without even trying, she was walking sex, not in a slutty, look-at-me way, but just by virtue of breathing. Or maybe that was just … her. What he knew of her. What he admired about her and wanted to know even better.

He definitely wanted to know Mariah better. All of her. Inside and out.

She was turning heads, causing a small scene among a group of college-age guys openly admiring her from the far corner. A few days ago, Sawyer had worried what others would think of him being with such a woman, had believed a prominent surgeon should have a conservative, less-noticeable woman on his arm. To hell with that. Now he wanted to be in the middle of her "scene."

The silent admission hummed through him like warm, soothing sunlight that heated him to the core, and just like that, things made sense. Everything. She might as well have been wearing one of those human sandwich board signs saying, *I'm what you need.*

"I'm turning down the job," he said to his mom, straightening from the wall.

"What?" Scandal rang through her voice. "You wanted it so badly, Sawyer. Why would you do that?"

He shook his head. "I wanted to want it. Wanted to make you proud. Wanted to, I don't know, overachieve or something. Like you and Rachel always do. But..." He watched Mariah as she greeted the rest of the group. "That's not me, Mom. I'm a simple guy. Happy with the job I have. Ready to make some other life improvements that have nothing to do with work."

When he glanced toward his mother, her mouth was open, jaw gaping. She tilted her head. "You thought ... you thought I wanted that for you? Like you're not good enough the way you are? Really?"

He considered her words, then shook his head. "Not really, I guess. You've never pushed me unreasonably. I think it's ... just me. I was trying to be the wrong guy. Not doing what I want with my life."

Jackie grasped his forearm. "That won't work, Sawyer." She shook her head adamantly, appearing to search for words. "That's..."

"A thing of the past," he said, his voice a little louder, conviction stronger. "It was stupid. Don't know what the hell was wrong with me, but I'm going to see about making some changes. I'll be back after while."

He was pretty sure his mom's mouth was hanging open again as he walked toward Mariah.

MARIAH SENSED Sawyer's approach more than saw it. She'd been hyperaware of him over there against the wall with his mom. Uber-aware of his presence, his every move.

Damn man.

She tried to avoid a random conversation with him by heading over to the wall of windows, acting like she was looking for the awaited plane. Of course, nothing with him had gone the way she'd wanted from the start, and he followed her now.

She leaned her forehead into the glass and held on to the black metal that separated the panes, hoping to discourage him.

"Mariah," he said in that low, delicious voice that did something to her whenever she heard it.

She steeled herself against that response. There was nothing left to discuss between them. "Excuse me." She looked past him and headed toward the women's restroom as a respite. She couldn't hide from him forever, but standing here in the middle of everyone, acting like there wasn't a problem... Not gonna happen.

Without looking back, she went into the restroom, relieved that it was nearly empty — not surprising since their gate was the last in a long terminal, and most of the traffic congested closer to the main part of the airport.

Mariah splashed water on her face, trying to regain her equilibrium. She'd been crushed by Sawyer's decision Friday. Way more crushed than the situation called for. They'd only really started getting to know each other ten days ago. Should be low stakes.

"Should" being the key word.

Ridiculously, emotion balled in her throat, and her eyes teared.

Anger. That's all it was. Anger and pride.

She went partway into one of the stalls and ripped off a length of tissue to dab at her eyes. Someone came into the restroom behind her, and she kept her back to the world as she regained her composure.

The person stopped behind her, she assumed at the sink or the mirror, and didn't seem to have any intention of moving, so when her eyes were clear, Mariah straightened and turned around. She promptly fell into the stall wall.

"No way... What the hell, Sawyer?"

"I know you don't want to talk to me, but hear me out. Please?"

"This is the ladies' room."

He glanced around uninterestedly. "We're alone, at least for the moment. I screwed up, Mariah. Big-time."

Oh, god. All kinds of things he could've said that wouldn't break her down, wouldn't soften her, and that was the one she couldn't walk away from. She met his eyes, his beautiful, intelligent, chocolate-brown eyes that conveyed so much determination right now.

"I was wrong. So one thousand percent wrong," he said.

"About?"

A woman sauntered into the restroom then, saw Sawyer, gasped, and froze in her tracks.

"Hi," Sawyer said. "Sorry. Can you give us five?"

"There's another women's room just down the way," Mariah told her, intrigued enough by Sawyer's beginning to not feel too badly about taking over the bathroom. Without thinking about it, she moved closer to Sawyer.

"Well," the woman spat. "I never!" But she turned on her heel and exited, leaving them alone once again.

"You were saying you were wrong about something," Mariah prompted him.

Falling deeply into thought, Sawyer strolled to the long vanity and leaned against it. "I'm not sure where to start."

"How about with your point."

"You," he said without hesitation. "You're the point. I like you, Mariah. A lot."

She frowned, crossing her arms over her chest. "You have a strange way of showing it."

A hint of a self-deprecating — endearing, dammit — grin tugged at his lips. "Fair enough. I'd like to get to know you better. I want a *relationship* with you. If you'll give me another chance."

Like it or not, she couldn't stop her heart from speeding up. But her brain wasn't as easy as her ticker. "Why the one-eighty?" she asked. "Why would I buy into such a turnaround?"

He trailed his finger across her still-crossed arm, and just that little touch sent a shiver through her. His grin reappeared, this time a sly version of it. "Because the sex was good?" he said in a husky voice.

The combo of contact, that voice, and the memory of being with him… Crap, she was going down in flames in record time.

"Good?" she asked, acting offended.

"Stupendous?"

"A little better." She had trouble wiping the smile from her lips.

Sawyer pried her stubborn arms apart and twined their fingers together. "Come here." He pulled her closer, so she was nestled between his legs. "I'm about to veer from the *How to Win Chicks* manual, just so you know."

"Okay…"

Their entwined hands were at shoulder level, and he leaned his forehead into hers. "Like I told you, probably in some drunken stupor last Saturday night, I come from a family of over-achievers," he said. "My mom is one of the best cardiologists in the state. She's been in charge of so many committees and organi-zations I can't keep track. Rachel, she's always been the best at everything she takes on. Emergency medicine is no exception. She's like a steamroller, barreling over every goal she sets. Even Noelle…" He hesitated at the name of his sister who'd died three years ago. "She was a social girl, but in her own way, she owned that. She had a billion friends. Everyone knew they could go to her with anything. She'd be there for them."

"I remember," Mariah said quietly. Before Rachel and Cale had gotten together, her brother had loved Noelle.

"So here's me, this eternal underachiever, I guess."

"You are not! You're a freaking surgeon, Sawyer. Last I checked, that's no small undertaking."

He pressed his lips together, considering. "Maybe. In normal families."

"I see where you're going with this. Your family isn't normal — not that there is such a thing — but it's tough to be surrounded by people like them."

"Yes. Without starting to feel like you need to be more your-self. Which is where the medical director of surgery job at St.

Mary's comes in. I thought that's what I should want. That and dedicating myself to being a focused, responsible 'grown-up.' You know, someone who doesn't wake up naked in some gorgeous woman's bed."

"Gorgeous?"

"Understatement," he said, his voice turning gravelly.

"Truth? I kind of liked having you wake up in my bed naked."

"I more than kind of liked it … or would have if I'd let myself. I'm still embarrassed about it."

"Well, don't be." Mariah let her face drift closer to his. "So, go on."

Sawyer shrugged. "That's what I was wrong about. I don't want any of that. I love my 'lowly' general surgeon job. I'd be happy to retire from it in thirty years. I want to be a part of the community, keep running into my patients when I'm out, and…"

"And?"

"I want to date whoever the hell I want to, whenever I want to, and spend as much time with a particular redhead as is humanly possible. *If* she feels the same. So here I am … in the women's restroom at the airport groveling."

"It's a little lacking in ambience, but I have to admit, it's kind of *flattering* that you hunted me down in here."

"Kind of?"

"Stupendously flattering," she whispered as she closed the remaining space between their mouths.

"Excuse me," a woman's voice said as she rounded the corner into the restroom.

"Don't mind us," Sawyer said before returning to Mariah's lips.

"Don't mind me," the woman said, barreling into the first stall. "I gotta go."

Mariah laughed and ran her finger over her lips. "Come on," she whispered to Sawyer. "We have a plane to meet and a date — or a hundred — to go on."

She pulled him behind her out of the bathroom. They'd made

it several yards, hand in hand, toward the gate when his mom rushed by and then stopped as she recognized them.

"There you two are! You missed everything! We're all heading to the airport tavern for a drink to celebrate."

Mariah looked up at Sawyer to see how he was going to play this. He peered down at her and they shared a knowing grin.

"Okay, then," he said to his mom as he gazed at Mariah. "We'll join you. Personally, I think the best part is yet to come."

Jackie looked from her son to Mariah. With a sparkle in her eye, she nodded her understanding before preceding them toward the bar.

Sawyer gave Mariah's hand a squeeze as they followed his mom.

"Our first official date," she said.

"Pre-date," Sawyer corrected. "I'll try to have you home by sun-up."

SLOW BURN

AN ISLAND FIRE SHORT STORY

ABOUT SLOW BURN

They've both dug their roots deep…eight hundred miles apart.

Zoe Griffin has a fresh new life—a hard-earned doctorate degree and a burgeoning nutritionist practice in Colorado. The only thing missing is the man she fell in love with.

Cooper Flannagan did "new life" ad nauseam as an Army brat and shudders at the very mention of change. His fellow firefighters on San Amaro Island, Texas, are his family. He's dug his roots deep, and he finally feels like he belongs. But can he ever be truly content without the woman he loves?

Slow Burn is a stand-alone short story with a four-alarm happy ever after in the Island Fire series. Zoe and Cooper first appeared in *Up in Flames*.

1

Cooper Flannagan would know that voice anywhere.

It was the voice of an angel. Scratch that. The voice of a siren. The voice of his ex-girlfriend, Zoe Griffin, who also happened to be the sister of his roommate, Penn.

He rolled over in his king-size bed, his sleep-blurred mind wondering how the hell he could've passed out so hard after his shift that he would miss his alarm. It'd been a rough shift, for damn sure — he could still smell the acrid smoke odor from the apartment fire even though he'd showered twice — but he felt like he'd just fallen asleep minutes ago.

He reached over to the nightstand and fumbled around for his phone to check the time. *One o'clock?* Zoe and her mother weren't supposed to arrive from Colorado until after four p.m. He'd planned to be out of the condo by then.

Cooper turned onto his stomach and shoved his head under his pillow in an attempt to block out that laugh of hers. That melodious sound that used to make his world go round. He needed more than four hours' sleep in order to survive the next four days with Zoe in town.

It was no use. He lay there for the longest ten minutes of his life, fighting to go back to slumberville, but he couldn't stop imagining every move she might be making, the way the waves in her shiny, brunette hair sometimes fell into her face as she spoke, what she might be wearing…

He'd known there was no way to avoid her this weekend, but he'd hoped he could put off running into her at least until tomorrow. Her surprise early visit had ruined that.

She had to know he was here. Penn would tell her even if she didn't ask. Did that mean… Did she *want* to see him?

The thought was more enticing than he'd ever admit out loud. And it had him sitting up on the edge of the bed, unable to ignore the burning curiosity any longer. Because suddenly, despite what he'd been telling himself and the rest of the world the four months since they'd broken up, he wanted more than anything to see Zoe.

ZOE CUT off her own sentence halfway through and promptly forgot what she was saying. Forgot she was saying *anything*. That's what seeing Cooper in the flesh did to her.

He'd slipped into the bathroom from his bedroom — his shaggy, golden-brown head had only been in her line of sight for two-point-two seconds max — and she lost all track of the conversation with her mom and brother. Lucky thing that breathing was involuntary, otherwise she probably would have forgotten that too.

And this was after three weeks of preparing herself, of imagining the moment she laid eyes on him again, knowing she would see him lots over the course of her big brother's birthday weekend. Almost a month of visualizing it having *no effect whatsoever on her*.

Yeah, so much for visualization.

"You didn't tell me he was here," she hissed at her knucklehead brother.

"He lives here, Zo."

Was that a smirk on Penn's face? Definitely a spark of amusement in his green eyes. She managed to swallow the urge to throttle him and bit the inside of her lip until it bled.

Their mother, Nell Griffin, who was sitting with her back to the hallway, looked around curiously. "Is Cooper home?"

"He's sleeping," Penn said.

"*Was* sleeping," Zoe clarified.

"He worked last night."

Which meant he'd finished his shift at the fire station at seven this morning, Zoe knew. Then he'd likely gone out for breakfast with the guys he'd worked with — scrambled eggs, thick-cut bacon, and enough greasy hash browns with cheese to stop a weaker heart were his favorites — then straight home to sleep. He'd probably stripped down to nothing and climbed into the cool sheets of the king-size bed he'd no doubt made the previous time he'd crawled out of it.

Zoe shook her head to erase the details she knew so well. Especially the naked bit.

"You can't be surprised, honey," their mom said.

No. Surprised wasn't it. Leveled by fresh pain was more like it. Four months of trying to get over Cooper, trying to get on with her life, and the sting was as acute in this moment as it had been the night they'd argued long-distance — ironically, about their long-distance relationship status — and then broken up. That she'd been the one to end it made no difference whatsoever.

Her throat felt like a ball of felt had lodged in it, and her mouth had become instantly parched.

"I'm going to get that water you offered me after all," she said to Penn as she stood. If she was in the kitchen, she wouldn't be able to see when Cooper emerged from the bathroom and went back to bed. She glanced at her watch. "Then we should head to the Silver Sands and check in, Mom."

"Check-in isn't usually until three or four." Nell frowned and tilted her perfectly coiffed head at her daughter as Zoe headed toward the kitchen.

"We know the owner," she said over her shoulder in an understatement. "I'm sure Nadia will get us in whenever we're ready."

Zoe was so ready.

And so too slow.

She heard footsteps behind her as she stood at the sink filling a glass. Bare footsteps. Not her brother, as he wore shoes most of the time to help support his back after the injury that had ended his firefighting career. Not her mother, as noisy heels were permanently attached to her feet.

Keeping her back to the doorway, Zoe turned off the tap and brought the glass to her dry lips. The glass was too small, the water gone too fast, as Cooper stood several feet behind her at the breakfast bar. Waiting. She could feel his stare on her back.

"Hey," he finally said when she continued to stall with her back to him. "Zoe."

She closed her eyes. There was a certain timbre in his voice whenever he spoke her name. A slight drawl to the "oh" sound in it. She'd always loved it.

Now it made her want to cry.

Swallowing that urge back, she set the empty glass in the sink and turned around, not meeting his eyes. Afraid to let herself gaze into those blue eyes she'd loved. Afraid to discover whether his love was still there, reflecting back at her.

"You look good," he said. "Really good."

At the hint of a grin in his voice, her eyes rose to his face. Two days' growth shadowed his jaw, and she could recall exactly how that stubble felt on her skin. Rough but not painful. Undeniably masculine. His dirty-blond hair was a mess, even though he couldn't have slept that long. Then she made the mistake of meeting his gaze. The pain zapped her like a shock of static electricity directly to her heart.

She so couldn't do this.

Averting her eyes, she did the only thing she could handle, immature or not, and made a beeline for the living room.

"Why do you have to be this way, Zoe?" His words, soft, achingly vulnerable, stopped her as she was about to hit the doorway to the other room.

Instinct and habit urged her to run into his arms the way she always had whenever they saw each other after weeks apart. She stood there, back to him once again, fighting that instinct, imagining her feet planted in the sand against the pull of the waves in the gulf. Reminding herself of why they weren't together anymore. Why it would never work between them.

"Just … just don't, Cooper. Please." She swallowed hard and took a good three seconds to blank her face before walking out to the living room and picking up her purse from the floor. "Penn, are you coming with us to the hotel?"

"You know it." He rose eagerly, no doubt motivated by the fact that Nadia, the woman he planned to propose to this weekend, would likely be there.

Zoe was ecstatic for him and adored Nadia, but at this particular second, the love in his expression was in stark contrast with the heartbreak throbbing through her.

"We need to go. Please."

2

———————

Cooper's dart hit the three, and the bitch of it was, the damn thing was right up against the outer bull's-eye ring. Touching it. So close in distance but so far from that twenty-five points. Just like he was with Zoe.

He went to the full-sized, bar-style dart cabinet that he'd splurged on right after he and Zoe had called it quits — now the centerpiece of the living room — and plucked out his darts. He set his feet behind the strip of duct tape they'd stuck down on the tile floor a precise seven feet and nine and a quarter inches away. Muttering a vulgar threat to the state-of-the-art board, he let another dart fly just as the front door opened behind him.

Like a dumb ass, his heart sped up with hope that it was Zoe, even while his brain knew full well it was Penn. He grunted at his roommate and tossed another dart, nailing the three.

"Stiff competition?" Penn asked, tossing his keys on the end table and giving Cooper adequate space to finish his turn before going to the cabinet and retrieving his own set of darts.

"I'm off my game tonight. How was dinner?"

"As good as it can be with three gabby women." Penn's love-drunk grin contradicted the exasperation in his tone.

"You think Nadia has any idea you're gonna pop the question?"

"She was so busy chattering about the details of my party I'm pretty sure she's oblivious."

"Excellent," Cooper said. "Where'd you eat?"

"Went to Local Lou's. My mom loves that place."

"You mean Zoe loves it." She'd insisted on eating there every single time she'd been in town. Cooper had always been happy to comply. It was decent food, especially for being "healthy," but even better was making Zoe content. Nothing selfless about it on his part — he loved seeing her face light up, watching her enthusiasm over something as simple as a local-ingredient salad.

"Wasn't sure I was allowed to mention her name around you."

"Don't be a jerk-off." Cooper reset the game — not a sacrifice as crappy as he'd been doing — and pushed the two-player option.

"Heard you after we walked out the door earlier," Penn said.

Shit. Watching Zoe and her family walk out without him, even though he wouldn't have joined them if they'd asked, had pissed Cooper off irrationally. Like an overgrown four-year-old, he'd smacked the closed door behind them. And maybe yelled a couple of choice swear words to the empty condo.

He said nothing as Penn took his turn.

"This is why people don't break up on the phone," Penn said as he pulled the darts off the board.

"Wasn't my doing."

"You don't have closure that way. Then the next time you run into each other…" Penn shook his head.

"Tell your sister that."

"Tell her yourself."

"She doesn't want anything to do with me." Cooper threw the first dart of his turn so hard it bounced off the board and skidded across the slick floor.

"Seems like you want something to do with her."

Cooper gritted his jaw — hard — on the urge to tell his roommate to fuck off. Reining in the need to smash the darts into the board, he managed to toss the next one gently enough to stick in the triple one.

"You can tiptoe around each other all weekend, I guess," Penn said at the exact moment Cooper threw his third dart, distracting him just enough that he hit the bull's-eye. Fucking figured.

Cooper walked to the board and slowly plucked out his darts. "You think I should get my 'closure.'" He moved off to the side.

"What I really think you should do?" Penn tossed in a triple twenty. "Both of you should quit being so damn hardheaded."

Coop let out a sardonic chuckle. "Good luck with that. Your sister is the most stubborn woman I've ever known."

"Two peas in a pod." Penn continued to nonchalantly kick Cooper's ass with a bull's-eye.

Cooper told him where to go.

"What do you want from her, Coop? You wanna get back together?"

"Two people have to want that for it to happen, dude."

"Answer the question."

Cooper took his entire turn without saying a word. Did he want Zoe back? God, he'd loved her. More than he'd loved anyone in his thirty-five years. But it was past tense, love with an *ed* on the end. Getting back together? He wasn't going there. Not an option.

"I want her to not hate me," he said quietly. How the hell had it come to them not being able to say *hello, how are you* to each other?

"So go do something about it. I'm destroying you so completely at darts it's getting embarrassing anyway."

Cooper narrowed his eyes at his roommate, not sure which of his statements pissed him off more. He shook his head. Penn was right about both.

Dammit.

He slammed his darts down on the table by Penn's keys, felt for his own keys in his front pocket, and headed for the door. "Don't wait up."

Zoe paced from one end of the hotel room to the other, bathroom to balcony door, as her mother crawled under the covers of one of the beds.

"You okay?" her mom asked.

Pausing at the balcony door, Zoe moved the curtain aside and looked out at the waves in the moonlight. She would never get tired of the sight — Nadia had set them up with a primo view — but tonight, neither it nor the normally soothing roar was doing a thing to relieve Zoe's agitation.

"Just restless," she said as she considered sitting out on the balcony for a few. She shook her head. Sitting still, trying to relax sounded like torture.

"You should've taken Nadia up on the offer to have a drink in the bar."

"I almost did. But I was afraid I'd say something to give away Penn's secret. I nearly slipped up three or four times at dinner."

"Heavens, me too. Just one more day to get through without blowing it, thank goodness."

Zoe's phone vibrated on the nightstand between the two beds, and she went to it, hoping for a text from one of her friends from home, any of them, to distract her.

Her heart dipped into her stomach when she saw Cooper's name on her phone.

You awake? the text message read.

Zoe let out a frustrated breath.

"Who is it?" Nell asked.

"Three guesses." She returned the phone to the nightstand and went back to the balcony door, needing the physical distance from Cooper and his message.

"Cooper?"

Zoe didn't answer.

"You're being kind of hard on him, aren't you?" Her mom's voice was gentle, more sympathetic than her words, and tears threatened in Zoe's eyes.

"Not on purpose. I just..." She shook her head. "It's tougher than I expected."

The phone buzzed again. Another message. Zoe fought the need to check what it said.

She sensed her mom watching her, felt her mother's sympathy reaching out to her as if it had fingers. Zoe swiped the tears away.

"Have you ever given serious thought to moving here, Zoe? To be with him—"

"Of course I have! A thousand times." Zoe swallowed down the pulsing lump in her throat. "I can't do it, Mom. Not in good conscience. After everything Celeste and the others have done for me, allowing me to start building my name even before I was officially done with school, I can't just walk away from my job. It'd put them in a bind just as much as it would mean starting from scratch for me, and financially, I don't have the years it would take to build up a new following."

"They have been extremely good to you," her mom admitted.

"I saw what it did to the clinic when David Jennings moved to Chicago. The other two ended up working sixty-hour weeks to handle his clients as well as their own. Until I could step in and officially start taking some of them over. And they trusted me to do that, Mom." Zoe knew her voice was much too emotional, loaded with defensiveness, but how could her mom even ask her this stuff? She of all people *knew*. "I'm five years ahead of where I'd be otherwise."

"It'd be bad to leave them in the lurch after all their support," Nell acknowledged.

"I wouldn't be able to forgive myself."

"Do you think," her mom said, "it might be a good idea for you and Cooper to deal with this awkwardness now, so you don't ruin your brother's big weekend?"

Her words were like a jab to Zoe's chest. That was the one thing her mom could say to make her back down. Zoe wanted Penn's weekend to be amazing. He deserved it, especially after all the suffering he'd gone through because of his back injury.

Inhaling a deep, unsteady breath, she willed the tears away. She marched to the nightstand and picked up the phone, turning away from her mom for privacy.

Would like to talk sometime. Settle the air, Cooper's text said.

Zoe bit her lip. Closed her eyes hard. Summoned her big-girl panties and replied:

Meet me on the beach in ten.

3

Cooper's stomach was in a knot. Which was stupid when he thought about it. So Zoe was on her way outside to talk to him. So what? They were over. History. His gut shouldn't be all tied up just to talk to her. If she couldn't treat him decently, what was it to him?

Yeah. He could keep telling himself that until the waves stopped beating the shore and it still wouldn't be true.

At this point, he'd be lucky if she showed up. It'd been twelve minutes since she'd said ten.

He made a point of watching the water, of keeping his back to the hotel where Zoe would come from. Though it was nearly ten thirty and dark, the beach was relatively busy for the hour, with groups and couples wading and splashing, trying to find relief from the hotter-than-usual Texas summer night. They'd be better off inside by the air conditioner — there was hardly any breeze coming off the water.

"Sorry I'm late." Zoe came up next to him and startled him, even though he'd been waiting for her. She held out a bottle of beer to him — his usual brand, just the way he liked it. In her other hand was a tall, skinny glass with a light-colored liquid in it and a drink umbrella and straw sticking out.

"Thanks," Cooper said before taking a healthy swig. The ice-cold brew hit the spot, and it couldn't hurt to relax him a bit. "What's in yours? Green tea?"

Zoe wasn't much of a drinker. The health freak in her didn't sit well with putting alcohol into her body, but every once in a great while, she'd imbibe. Though her dedication to all things health and nutrition had puzzled him at first, it was one of the things he'd grown to love about her — her steadfastness to her beliefs. Of course, that was closely related to her stubbornness...

"Margarita," she said after a sip. "Bartender was out of margarita glasses."

She needed alcohol to talk to him. Cooper closed his eyes and clenched his jaw as that sank in.

Zoe walked a couple dozen feet toward the waterline and sat down in the dry sand, giving Cooper little choice but to follow. He sat, raised his knees, and braced his elbows on them as the heavy brininess of the air rolled over him.

He watched her profile out of the corner of his eye as the silence between them expanded. She lifted her straw to her lips, and he couldn't prevent the pang in his chest at the thought of those lips and how familiar they'd once been to him and with him.

"I miss you, Zoe," he said without hesitation. Judging by the way her eyes slammed shut, he should have hesitated.

"Let's not go there. There's no use."

"What happened to us? We were so close, and now we sit here a foot apart on the beach, but it's like we've got a football field between us."

She turned her head partway toward him. Her eyes were downcast and so damn sad it took every thread of willpower he could muster not to reach out and brush his fingers over her cheek.

"*Were* close," she said. "Past tense. We weren't meant to be, Cooper. We're going in two different directions."

"Are we?"

Her lids lowered, and her long lashes sparkled in the moonlight. Tears?

Shit. Please, no tears.

"We've been over this, Coop. So many times. My life is in Boulder. I can't leave my clinic — you know what they did for me and how they helped me. And your life is here on the island."

He'd hoped so hard when she'd finished her doctorate last summer that she would consider moving to San Amaro and starting out her nutritionist career here. He understood about the contacts and the partners she'd joined who'd bent over backwards for her. Understanding didn't make it any easier.

"You love it here, though," he said, knowing it was a weak argument.

"I do. But it doesn't matter. I can't move here, and you made it clear where you stand when you chose San Amaro over me."

"I never—" He shook his head, reeling. Chose San Amaro over her?

"Did you not tell me your career is here?"

"Yeah." His career and, even more important, his home. "Zoe, you know how much my family moved me around when I was a kid. When my dad finally retired from the military and moved us here, one last uprooting, I swore to myself I would die here—"

Zoe put her hand on his thigh. "I know, Cooper." She nodded sadly. "I get it." Her tone, though gentle, said that was that.

Was it? Was their breakup solely his fault? She'd never asked him outright to move to Colorado, and he'd never seriously considered it ... because of his vow to himself as a teenager tired of not fitting in, of not belonging.

He belonged here. The fire department was his family, his only family now. He owned a condo on the beach, owned it outright, thanks to his parents.

He couldn't fathom leaving all this behind. Could he?

She turned her head the rest of the way to meet his gaze. "I'm here because I don't want the awkwardness between you and me to affect Penn."

"So how do we make it not awkward? I don't want you to hate me, Zo."

She dropped her hand from his leg and looked out at the gulf. "I don't hate you." Her voice was thick, lower than normal. "I could never hate you. It might be easier if I could."

Without warning, she stood, then took a long sip of her drink. Cooper got up too, feeling lost. Hopeless.

"Too much tequila in this," Zoe said with a shudder. "Want it?" She held out the glass.

He took it from her, having no intention of drinking it.

"So…" he said, wanting to say so much but not having a damn clue where to start.

"So … peace? We can act normal for three days, can't we?"

"Normal?" Normal between them had always been *together*, from the first day he'd met her, when she'd showed up for a surprise visit after Penn's back surgery.

"We can get along, I mean."

"We always have." Except when the question of long-term plans came up.

Zoe nodded once. "It'll be okay. We can both do this for Penn. That's what's important, right?"

Being able to talk like this was important. Cooper shrugged and attempted a nod, because God knew there were other things that were important too. Like being able to breathe — and right now, he was having a hard time with that.

As Zoe brushed her hands together to get rid of the sand, he struggled to come up with a stall, something to prolong their time together tonight, but … they weren't together anymore. She was just his roommate's sister now. Not even really someone he could call a friend … and yet so much more.

"Thanks for coming out here, Zo," he said, refusing to voice agreement with her last statement. He nodded and swallowed hard against the dread of walking away from her. "Guess I'll see you tomorrow."

4

―――――――――

"What the hell are you doing out here at this hour?" Cooper slowed from a jog to a walk as he approached the beach side of the fire station. His friend and colleague Nate Rottinghaus was hollering at him from the patio, most likely waiting for the end of his shift at seven o'clock.

"I'd ask you the same, but you're a freak of nature," Cooper said. Nate was notorious for his up-at-the-butt-crack-of-dawn ways.

Cooper went over and collapsed on the lounger next to Nate's.

"Didn't know you liked to run on the beach," Nate said.

"*Like* is a strong word."

Nate studied him with narrowed eyes and then nodded knowingly. "Zoe got to town, huh?"

Cooper shrugged.

"Like hell you don't know. I take it it isn't going well?"

Cooper watched a tourist with a surfboard trying to navigate the small waves. San Amaro wasn't known for surfing, but travelers boarded up anyway, determined to singlehandedly change that.

"We worked it out," he finally said.

"*Worked it out* worked it out? Got back together?"

"Oh, hell no. Made it so we can be in the same room together."

"Good plan. So is that it? As good as it's gonna get?"

"Looks like it."

"You just gonna let it go at that, man?" Nate leaned forward and put a foot down on each side of the lounge chair. "Let the girl of your wet dreams walk away?"

"You always an asshole this early in the morning?"

Nate chuckled. "That non-answer speaks volumes."

Outside of Penn, Nate was probably the best friend Cooper had. Nate's dad, Ed, was a lieutenant in the department, and the two single Rottinghauses often had Coop and anyone else without family to their house for holidays. The bitch of it was that, consequently, Nate knew him well and didn't hesitate to call his bullshit.

Cooper figured swearing at him some more would just fuel the fire, so he stood, went to the charcoal grill, and pushed around the cool ashes with one of the barbeque tools. He tried to blank his mind, but Nate's words about letting it go wouldn't leave him alone.

Was he going to leave it be? Let Zoe go for good?

Could he?

He hadn't slept more than a couple of hours last night, and those had been restless, dream-filled sons of bitches. No mystery why that was. He'd walked away from her on the beach, tried like hell not to look back, but failed. Just as he'd gotten to the corner of the building, he'd turned around for one last glimpse. He'd caught Zoe watching him, at which point she'd given a minute shake of her head and turned away with purpose.

No.

He wasn't done.

After thinking about nothing else all night and being unable to erase her from his brain on a run this morning, the truth became apparent to him.

It was better to have a little bit of Zoe, for a short time, than no Zoe at all.

Sᴜɴsʜɪɴᴇ. Sea air. Sharks.

The first two were no-brainers for Zoe. The third was a little out of her comfort zone, but bragging rights were at stake today.

She led her mom toward where the *Shark Whisperer* was docked. The *Whisperer* and its crew were going to take them on an all-day deep-sea fishing excursion, and Zoe was going to do everything in her power to catch a shark, mostly because Penn thought he could outdo her. As they'd discussed possible activities for today last night at dinner, they'd done what any siblings would do — they'd placed a bet. Whoever caught a shark first won bragging rights and dinner. Their mom had gotten in on it as well, surprising the heck out of Zoe, but she had to admit, this relatively new closeness their family of three had developed since Penn's back injury was what she'd longed for since, well, probably since her dad had left them so many years ago. It'd just taken them a few too many years and a serious medical emergency to accomplish it. Nadia had gradually become part of it from time to time as she and Penn had grown closer, but she couldn't get away from her job at her family's hotel today, so the three Griffins were on their own.

Or so Zoe'd thought.

Why was Cooper here with Penn?

As Zoe and her mom approached the dock, the two men were talking to a couple of guys on the boat, laughing it up like nothing was wrong. Zoe faltered as she fought not to stop altogether and turn around. She hoped like hell she pulled it off as Cooper noticed her and grinned. She could swear there was an edge of smugness to that grin.

Rat bastard.

She was not going to let him see she was shaken by his presence.

"Are we late?" her mom asked as one of the two guys wearing *Shark Whisperer* caps met them at the plank to embark.

"Nah. You're fine," Penn said. "I'm sure you girls needed to rest up to have a snowball's chance in hell at reeling in a fish big enough to keep."

Zoe raised her chin in challenge. "Keep talking smack, big shot. We'll see who wins. As long as these guys weren't giving you any unfair advantages." She gestured to the two crew members.

"Nope. Gully and I graduated from high school together," Cooper said. "Nothing to feel threatened about. I'm here as a neutral third party."

Two sentences had never been more contradictory.

Zoe didn't even have to look directly at Cooper to feel threatened — concerning not the shark bet but her equilibrium. Her mental health. Her good mood.

"Hi. Sam Gulliver," one of the guys, whose shirt read *Captain* over the pocket, said, holding his hand out to her. "You can call me Gully. Welcome aboard."

"Thank you. Which one of you is going to help me beat my brother at catching the first shark?"

"That'd be me." The second guy, who'd been bent over one of the supply boxes, stood and approached their group. "Adam Valdez. I'm your fishing guide, a.k.a. shark-catching expert."

"A.K.A. lead bullshitter," the captain said, the corners of his eyes crinkling in good humor and a little sun damage.

Shark expert, bullshitter, and God's gift to women, Zoe thought as Adam took her hand in more of a welcoming grasp than a shake. He had the kind of bright blue eyes that cut through the logic sections of a woman's brain and went straight to her instinct, whether dormant or not, to bear beautiful babies. Fortunately, Zoe's instincts were wrapped up in the man three feet away, but she couldn't help being charmed around the edges when Adam continued to hold on to her hand and put his other one at her waist as she stepped onto the boat.

When Adam finally let go, reassuring her the whole time that she would do just fine at the fish pursuit, Zoe caught Cooper staring at them. Not smiling. When he realized she was looking back at him, he quickly glanced away and forced a too-jolly smile as he helped Zoe's mom onto the boat. Zoe couldn't deny his veiled jealousy stoked a glimmer of satisfaction. Enough of a glimmer that she didn't stop Adam when he insisted on helping her with her lifejacket and on her joining him at the bow as the captain finalized preparations and a woman with a matching *Shark Whisperer* T-shirt worked onshore to send their private fishing party off.

5

Forty-five minutes later, the captain cut the engine, and he and Adam sprang into action readying supplies. Zoe was still by herself in the front, thankful for the illusion of physical separation from Cooper, who was in the back of the boat with the others, and grasping it for as long as she could get away with it. Which turned out to be less than five minutes.

"Beautiful Zoe, come choose your weapon," Adam called.

The inappropriate thrill at the compliment died instantly when Zoe caught the expression on Cooper's face as she made her way to the main part of the deck, where everyone else was gathered. Not anger or jealousy. Just … sadness in his downcast eyes as he avoided her and stepped to the opposite side.

She was such a sap. She shouldn't let him get to her so easily. They were over, over, over. Biting her lip and summoning her protective shell so he wouldn't get to her, she went over to Adam and listened as he briefly explained the pros and cons of each fishing pole. And here she'd thought they were just poles.

"Which one has caught the most sharks?" she asked.

Adam took a hard look at her, his sea-blue eyes sparkling in amusement.

"Bringing in a shark can wear a two-hundred-fifty-pound muscle man out. Are you sure you're up for it?"

Zoe wasn't sure she was up for anything now, but she nodded. "Bring it."

"I'd suggest this pole. Strong yet light."

Penn and their mom selected poles, and Adam helped them bait them and choose a spot. Zoe went to one of the back corners of the boat and cast her line out, drawing on vague memories of fishing with her best friend, Lisa, as a kid in Colorado.

Cooper came over and sat on the bench seat across from hers.

"You're not fishing?" she asked, wondering why the heck he'd come if he wasn't going to put a line in.

He shook his head. "I'm Penn's backup. He's worried his back won't take it if he gets something big."

Alarm shot through Zoe. She hadn't considered that fishing could be tough on the back. "Good idea." She glanced over at her brother with concern. "Do you think these seats will be okay for him? We'll be out here for a long time."

"He'll be fine. He's a big boy."

"With a bad back."

"He knows how to take care of himself."

She nodded and turned back toward the water, knowing Cooper was right. Thankful someone was in tune with her brother's weakness.

The gulf was calm this far out — San Amaro Island was barely visible and only if you knew where to look — and the boat was fairly steady, with only a periodic dip here and there. There were no clouds in the sky, and the sun beat down directly, making Zoe glad she'd slathered on sunscreen before putting on her swimsuit, tank top, and shorts. She felt a drop of sweat trailing down between her breasts and pulled her tank over her head, fighting to ignore that Cooper was so close and staring at her bikini top. It was too hot to be modest with an ex. He'd seen it all before in every possible way.

When he walked away, she breathed a little more deeply, but her relief was short-lived. He returned and held out a bottle of ice-cold water for her and opened a can of beer for himself.

"Thank you," she said as she twisted the lid off and closed

her eyes at the coolness of the liquid on her tongue. She could feel Cooper still watching her from the side.

"You really are beautiful, Zoe," he said in a low voice only she could hear.

She paused with the bottle halfway to her lips. Squeezed her eyes shut as so many different emotions nailed her at once. Trying to cut off the longing that compressed her heart, she took a drink and searched her brain for a strategy. A way to cope, to get through this day. She felt trapped. Water stretched out around them in every direction, as far as she could see, and there was no way to avoid Cooper's sneak attack, no place to hide, other than the compact restroom in the cabin of the boat that Gully had mentioned earlier.

Her gaze trained on the distant horizon, she said through clenched teeth, "*Friends*, Cooper. Nothing more."

"Yeah, that's not really working for me."

"You have to make it work. We agreed. For Penn."

His brows contracted, and he shook his head, and though he tried to hide it, the hurt was there in his eyes again before he took a gulp of beer and walked away.

The relative solitude he left her in on her corner of the deck was anything but peaceful.

HOURS LATER, Cooper was as stretched out at the bow of the boat as he could be, on a long, curved bench seat. The height of the cabin and bridge provided a patch of shade and minimal relief from the sun's powerful beams, but he was still downing cold liquids — he'd switched to water after a single beer — one right after another.

His position not only afforded him one of the only places on the deck to really recline but he also had a perfect view of Zoe. Covertly, of course, because she'd made it clear she was not in the mood for him. Convincing Penn to bring him along had been a bad idea, but now he was stuck for another few hours.

Sharks had so far eluded their group, but they'd caught

enough fish to feed the town of San Amaro for a weekend. Big, ugly things. Penn had the biggest so far, a thirty-pounder that had fought him for a good half hour as he brought it in. His bull-headed friend had done it without Cooper's help, insisting that his back was fine, so Cooper hadn't done much of anything all day except piss off Zoe.

He was debating letting his eyes close for a few when he noticed Zoe sway and then sit down hard. Fairly certain the boat had remained steady and hadn't caused it, Cooper sat up, his eyes openly trained on her now, sensing something was off. Her back was to him, though, and he couldn't tell jack from here.

Cooper stood and casually stretched his arms over his head as he watched. She rolled her half-empty water bottle across her forehead and then, fishing pole braced between her knees, she dropped her forehead to her hand. Just hot or something more?

Before he could act, she grabbed her pole with both hands and stood. The end of the pole curved under the weight of some-thing pulling on the other end. Judging by the bend and the way Zoe braced her feet, she had something sizable — and strong. Shark?

Forgetting the possibility that she didn't feel well and the certainty that she didn't want his help, Cooper made his way to her corner of the deck. She didn't spare him a look, her full concentration on holding on to the rod. Every few seconds, she was able to reel the line in a bit, and then whatever was below would send a message that it wasn't going down easily.

"Feisty one," he said, knowing better than to utter the words *if you need help, I'm here.*

Her eyes determined and not leaving the U at the end of her pole, she said, "It's my shark. I can tell."

She struggled to hold her own, then when the thing let up a little, she reeled in some slack on the line. Then she collapsed back on the seat with a gasp. "Cooper."

He took the rod she held toward him and trained his eyes on her.

"Shark!" she said, sounding panicked. "Please. Don't let it get away."

"Zoe, what's wrong?" he asked, doing his best to not lose ground with the fish while he assessed her state. Her face had lost all color, and sweat dotted her forehead. "Dizzy?"

In reply, she lowered her head between her knees.

"Gully!" Cooper hollered. "I think she's feeling faint."

Instead of Gully, Adam was by Zoe's side in a flash.

"I'll get her if you take this," Cooper said, thrusting the pole in Don Juan's direction.

"Cooper, please," Zoe pleaded, head still buried. "Get my shark."

"I'll take her inside," Adam said. "She needs water and to get out of the sun."

Zoe's mom crowded in on the other side of Zoe as Adam picked her up, and Cooper gritted his teeth, stuck with the damn shark.

"Deep breaths, sweetie," Mrs. Griffin said.

Within ten seconds, Cooper and Penn were alone on the deck, and the silence exploded in Cooper's ears. And then the shark, or whatever it was, asserted itself again, and Cooper's attention was one hundred percent back on the pole as he pushed Zoe's rejection out of his head. If she wanted him to catch this damn thing, he'd catch it.

6

Zoe sensed someone staring at her, so she opened her eyes.

Cooper. Of course.

She tried to summon some annoyance, but she was worn down. Tired of working so hard to be on guard around him.

Those eyes … she could see his worry in them. Worry and so much more. When they'd first gotten involved, he'd been so guarded. Reluctant to let himself care too much. She'd grown to understand him, to grasp the reasons he was like that, and he'd grown to be able to show her he loved her. To tell her, even, which she suspected had been harder still for him.

That love was there now, in his eyes, in his mannerisms as he stepped up to the side of the boat cabin's couch-like bench that was more comfortable than it looked.

"Zoe." His voice was rough around the edges. "You okay?"

Lying on her side, she straightened her legs so there was room for him to sit on the edge, near her waist.

"I'm fine. Hydrating." She pointed to the three empty water bottles on the little table by her head. "I just got overheated, I think."

Cooper sat, his hips brushing up against her body, his closeness stirring her blood like it shouldn't be stirred. Not when she'd nearly passed out just an hour ago. Not when they were supposed to be history.

His fingers brushed over her cheek so tenderly it made her ache.

"I was worried, Zo Zo."

The nickname he used only in private punched her in the chest. Made her heart dip and then speed up with its intimacy and familiarity. His fingers trailed down to grasp her hand. She must be more out of it than she thought, because she didn't have it in her to pull away. She curled her fingers around his, weak but content.

"I'm good now," she said as her lids drooped.

"I caught your fish. That bastard wasn't too hip on the idea of coming aboard, but we got him. Thirty-two pound something-or-other. You win for biggest catch of the day."

Alarm pulsed through her. "Something-or-other?"

Cooper nodded. "Big, nasty thing. Can't remember what Gully called it."

"It's supposed to be a shark."

"No sharks today. But you kicked Penn's ass in poundage."

"He won't buy my dinner for that."

"I'll buy you dinner."

As an only child, Cooper had never understood sibling rivalry. He didn't get that dinner wasn't the point. Winning was.

"I can buy my own dinner."

He wasn't looking directly at her, and she almost missed it, but it was there again — a flash of hurt. Not anger. Just hurt — the kind that penetrated every single cell. The kind she'd been wrestling with ever since the night they'd ended things four long months ago.

She couldn't let her guard down completely, but she couldn't be the cause of that kind of pain.

Zoe ran her fingers over his, taking comfort in the familiarity of them. Their strength. The little hairs on the backs of them that were lighter than the hair on his head. The callouses and sun-roughened skin.

"Cooper? I'm sorry if I upset you by talking to Adam for so long."

His eyes darted to hers, and he shrugged. "He lays it on pretty thick."

And she'd lapped it up. To get to Cooper? "He's hot, but I'm not attracted to him."

Cooper sized her up.

"At all," she confirmed.

He seemed to relax a notch, then he stood. Paced the short distance to the other side of the cabin and back. He sucked in a full breath and then let it out, studying the low ceiling as if it could explain the mystery of women and the universe to him. "Would it be so bad for us to spend time together while you're here, Zoe?" Before she could answer, he plowed on. "I miss you. Beyond all the other stuff between us, I like you. Like being with you. Could we maybe set aside the fact that we can't agree on the future, just for this weekend, and see if we can enjoy the present?"

Her heart lurched in temptation. Oh, to pretend that everything was okay between them. To have a slice of what they used to have... To be able to do that and then walk away again on Sunday when it was time for her and her mom to fly home...

She ached for it.

Swallowing hard, she sat up. "I don't think that's a good idea, Cooper." She picked up her water bottle and forced herself to down several gulps even though she felt like she was floating in thick liquid, moving in slow motion.

"We can do dinner with the family, like you planned," he said. "Then ... I don't know. Take a walk on the beach. Like we used to. In public, no strings attached, no expectations."

He was playing unfairly now. One of her favorite things to do with him — in public — was walk on the beach at night. She'd insisted on it nearly every night she'd visited. They'd logged a lot of miles and a lot of conversations about everything under the sun — or the moon. They'd shared everything. Something about walking side by side, as partners, equals, with the sound of the gulf giving the illusion you were in a bubble, separate from the rest of the world, made it easy to say anything. To admit things you'd never even spoken aloud before. To let another person know you as well as you knew yourself. To know the other person just as deeply.

"No," she said, shaking her head slowly but adamantly as she stood. "Dinner with you and the family is okay." *Safe.* "But I'll buy my own, and no walk."

He tilted his head and looked at her hard, as if trying to determine if he could wear her down. Get her to change her mind. The spark of determination in his eyes unnerved her, but he merely nodded.

"Dinner's a start. You ready to go back above?" He checked his watch. "We should be about twenty minutes from shore. We'll see if there's a shady spot for you."

Zoe nodded and preceded him without taking his offered hand. Another minute down here, alone with Cooper, and she was liable to do something stupid, like give in to temptation and allow herself to love him for one more weekend.

7

Zoe was an idiot a hundred times over.

Mistakes so far tonight: Wearing the short sundress and heels she knew Cooper loved on her, showing up for dinner with him and her family, ordering a second glass of wine. But her biggest and baddest screw-up was giving in to the walk on the beach with him.

And right now, she wasn't entirely sure she cared.

He'd been relaxed and charming throughout dinner. Not pressuring her in the least bit. Interacting with her family, reminding her of how engaging and caring he'd always been. Reminding her of all the reasons she'd fallen for him in the first place.

The faint moonlight from the sliver of moon and the din of the waves cast a spell over them now. A dangerous spell. They insulated her and Cooper from the universe as they walked, her shoes dangling from her hand and her feet bare, along toward the north end of civilization on the island. Gave them an illusion of being unaffected by any moment but the present. Made it tough to think about their past, irrelevant to consider the future.

When he'd taken her hand, she'd woven her fingers with his without hesitation, drawn in by the familiarity of his touch, his heat and strength. Some nights in the past, they'd been content to walk in silence, but tonight they'd talked nonstop, as if making up for lost time, reminding themselves of the ins and outs between them. Keeping it light, as if they were both afraid any deep topics would bring them back to their impasse.

They reached the dunes just outside of the city limits, where patches of sea grass became more prevalent and the waves always seemed a little wilder.

"Want to keep going?" Cooper asked.

She knew the island stretched for several more miles, but they'd never trekked much farther than this. Her blood heated as she thought about why they'd always been too impatient to keep walking, too in a hurry to get back to the privacy of Cooper's condo.

"It's safe, right?" There were no lights ahead. No development. No people. The darkness promised to protect them from the real world, to keep reality from infringing on them. Maybe it was that second glass of wine talking, but that's what Zoe longed for right now. Just a little more time without thinking, without worrying. Just ... being. With Cooper.

"Pretty much," Cooper said. "Except..."

"Except what?" A pulse of alarm beat through her chest.

"Well, there's that pack of werewolves that's been reported..."

A laugh escaped her. "Ooh, I've always wanted to see a werewolf. As long as it's not the kind that bites humans?"

"Never know." He looked down at her with a possessive grin. "Good thing you have a badass firefighter to protect you." He dragged her closer to his side as they kept walking.

"You need to work on your technique," she said, leaning her head against his shoulder. "The protect-you-from-werewolves thing is glaringly obvious."

"Damn. Out of practice, I guess. I had this hot chick for over a year, and I pretty much had to fight her off rather than lure her in."

She couldn't help smiling, caught up in the solid feel of him under her cheek, the clean, earthy scent of him, the lulling, low timbre of his voice. "No luring allowed."

She forced herself to straighten and lift her head from his

shoulder. The recognition that this was a stolen moment and that it would have to end soon nudged at her consciousness. She soaked in every detail, filing them away for later, when all she would have was the memory.

"What's that?" She stopped walking, her eyes trained on a spot in the water ahead of them. "The waves look like they're glowing."

Cooper made a deep sound of acknowledgement, of contentment. "Ahh. Magic," he said in a voice barely above a whisper.

"Werewolf magic?"

"Algae magic. It's the glowing algae. Probably from a red tide."

"It's blue, not red."

"It's a kind of algae that makes the water look red during the day. When there's a disturbance in the water at night, they put on a show."

As she watched, she noticed more faintly lit waves ahead of them. "That's amazing. Beautiful."

They walked another fifty yards or so in awed silence. Transfixed. Each glow started out as a thin blue outline of a forming wave, and as the water picked up momentum, the light show expanded with it, looking like a backlit waterfall, courtesy of mother nature.

They stopped and faced the water, with luminescent waves stretching up and down the shore in front of them.

"You've seen this before?" Zoe asked, her voice hushed.

"Been a long time. And never such a big display. The little algae guys must've known I was bringing someone special tonight."

She turned toward him to call his bullshit, and their heads were closer than she'd realized. There was just enough moonlight that she could see the heat in his eyes. His familiar, beautiful eyes. Without allowing herself to think, she stood on tiptoe and kissed him. Something about the otherworldly spectrum of blue, glowing waves made it seem appropriate to do something completely reckless, and she lost herself in the man she knew so well at the very first touch of their lips.

Cooper's arm was at her waist in a heartbeat, pulling her into his warmth, fitting her to his body as if she were born to be aligned to him. The yin to his yang.

When she expected him to deepen the kiss, he reined himself in, hesitated. Zoe dropped her shoes onto the sand and ran both her hands up underneath his shirt, kneading the muscles in his back, drinking in the feel of his skin. Cooper pulled away just enough to make eye contact, and the connection between them in that second was like nothing Zoe had ever experienced before. Intense. Intimate. And yet, at the same time, it was like coming home to her own bed after traveling. Comforting and comfortable. A respite. Her insides turned to liquid and then began a slow boil as Cooper breathed out shakily, as if he was in ecstasy and torment at once. His vulnerability in that moment drew her in, drove her to assuage all his doubts, to fulfill all his needs — and hers.

He leaned forward, closed that last inch again. Claimed her, with his mouth, his hands, and, Zoe knew instinctively, his heart. She sank into him, surrendered as if the spell of the night air and the magical glow in the water had erased all doubts from her mind.

Their kisses were filled with so much need, with a desperation like never before. Zoe fought to block out that nagging buzz in the deepest recesses of her mind that whispered this was the last time, that this was unwise.

Cooper solved the problem for her by driving her to distraction with his hands. He worked his fingers below the halter-top of her dress, his touch on her nipples sending a shock of need to her core. Hands dropping to his butt, she pulled him closer, gloried in the feel of his hardness where her pulse throbbed. The relief was fleeting though. Her body begged for more.

Cooper knew her well enough to read exactly what she needed. After spending some time teasing her nipples with his tongue, his lips returned to hers, and his fingers slid to her thighs and worked their way up beneath her dress. This short, sexy thing was exactly the right one to wear tonight after all, she decided. She was caught up in kissing him when she felt a tug at the side of her hip. It took a couple of seconds to realize Cooper had ripped her string bikini panties on one side and, judging by the trail of his hands, had the other side next on his agenda. In seconds, the warm breeze touched her skin where it shouldn't have, and she felt the hot moistness of her own body in response. In response to this man and his roving, knowing hands and lips.

"Cooper, we should—" She broke off with a gasp as he slipped a finger inside of her.

"Come here," he said, his voice thick and rough.

Right now, she'd follow him anywhere. Turned out she didn't have to, though, as Cooper picked her up, grasping her backside and guiding her legs to wrap around him.

He glanced around as if searching and then took her to a place on the sand, farther from the blue-lighted water, where the tall beach grass formed the illusion of a barrier on three sides of them. Zoe slid down his legs, seeking out his lips again and keeping their bodies nestled together where she throbbed for him, but even though his hands were still on her rear, drawing her as close as possible, the contact did nothing to assuage her ache. A needy whimper escaped from her as he trailed his tongue along her jawline to her ear.

She arched her head back as he kissed a trail along her neck, the heat of his lips stoking the fire of need down lower. His hands again found their way under her dress to her thighs and higher, searing her bare skin and drawing a moan from her.

"Zoe." He growled her name in her ear. "I need you. Right now."

8

"Where?" she managed, keenly aware that standing flush to him was not enough. Could never be enough to quell the ache deep at the apex of her thighs.

She felt his hand on her stomach, between them, then lower again. Heard the snap of his shorts release, then his zipper. Before she could say more, before she had the chance to push his shorts out of her way and touch him, he broke the contact between them and kneeled in front of her. He bunched her short skirt up just below her navel, baring her to the stars above. Zoe tensed in anticipation of his touch. Silently begged for it.

His tongue found the very spot that pulsed for him. She gasped his name, her knees nearly buckling. Without his firm grip of her backside, she would have slid to the sand in a puddle of need.

He teased her with his tongue, his touch tender and careful. Too careful.

"Cooper, you're killing me."

"Good," he said, the word vibrating against her skin.

She dragged her fingers through his hair and tried to convey her need by pulling him closer. She felt his wicked laughter teasing her flesh … his hand urging her legs farther apart … then his tongue flicking over the very heart of her, making her suck in her breath and nearly collapse. He took his sweet time exploring her, driving her wild, never quite giving her as much as she needed. On purpose, of course.

"When did you … turn in to a tease?"

His response was an indecipherable growl.

When she thought she was going to die, he lowered her so she was straddling his legs, and he leaned back on his feet to keep her rear off the sand. She made a mental note to thank him for that consideration later. When she could think straight.

Before he could find a new way to torment her, she kissed him and worked his shorts down a few inches. He groaned when she finally grasped him, and she grinned smugly as he met her gaze with heavy-lidded, lust-filled eyes. Her intent to repay his teasing with some of her own lasted only until she could feel the solid tip of him at her entrance. She slid him into her urgently, losing what little of her control remained, and closed her eyes at the ecstasy of him filling her once again. Loving the coarse moans she drew from him.

"God, Zo." She could hear the effort it took for him to form words as she moved her hips over him. "Missed this.... Missed you."

At this very second, she didn't know how she'd lived without this, but she bit down on the words. Lost herself in the building heat, in the slide of their sweat-covered bodies together, in the driving need for release.

Cooper knew her body well, knew how to play her, how to move, where to touch her to make her tingle and burn from her center right down to her toes. Judging by the earthy sounds he made and the words he breathed into her ear, she did the same for him.

Sensation took over all rational thought, and she gave herself over to him completely, until the pressure deep within burst in an explosion of exquisite pleasure. His grip on her tightened. He threw his head back, squeezed his eyes shut, and Zoe watched him come as her own body still contracted and hummed in blessed euphoria.

Cooper's eyes opened, and he smiled, catching his breath. "Still wow, that."

"Times one hundred," Zoe said.

His lips found hers again, and the kiss was full of so much tenderness it filled Zoe with a different kind of ache. One she couldn't think about right now. She willed herself to let go of the thoughts that threatened and to memorize every moment of his touch. The feel of his thumb resting gently beneath her chin. The roughness of his chin on her skin. His musky, masculine scent enveloping her like a familiar blanket.

He shifted so that he was lying on his back and Zoe was stretched on top of him, again protecting her from the sand, though her knees were starting to hurt as her blood returned to the rest of her body.

As reality gradually nudged at her, anxiety began to pulse through her. "We should get back. My mom is probably wondering why our walk is taking so long."

"Your mom isn't that naive," Cooper said with a hint of a smug grin.

"Even more reason." She was pretty open with her mom, open enough her mom was fully aware that Zoe should not be rolling around the sand with Cooper. It was disconcerting enough to admit it to herself.

Zoe stood and brushed sand off her body. Even though Cooper had shielded her from it as much as possible, it seemed to be everywhere, sticking to her moist skin in the humid night air.

"Where is my underwear?" she asked, glancing back at her shoes in the spot where they'd been when he'd disposed of it.

Cooper laughed, a low, gravelly, admittedly sexy, post-sex sound. "I think it's pretty much out of commission. I'll buy you more."

Shaking her head, Zoe said, "I don't need more. I just don't want to leave it on the beach."

"Taken care of." He indicated his front pocket. "I'll throw it away, unless you'd like it for a souvenir."

"You're twisted." She grinned in spite of her growing need to put distance between herself and what she'd let happen.

"You always liked that about me," Cooper said as he stood and put himself back together. "Among other things." His smile faded as he studied her. "Come here, Zo Zo."

He held out his hand for her to take. She looked down at it, doubts creeping in like a rogue spider taking over a shoe. Cooper stepped toward her, and she didn't have a chance at resisting. She wrapped her arms around him, drinking in his reassurance, believing, for the moments their bodies were entwined again, that everything was okay.

"Don't read too much into what just happened," she said into his shoulder.

He was still for several seconds, and then he nodded. "It is what it is." He dropped a kiss on her forehead and straightened. Sucked in a lungful of the thick air. "Ready?"

Shoving her misgivings away, Zoe nodded and took his hand, picked up her shoes, and they slowly made their way back to the real world.

9

By the time they could see the Silver Sands Hotel, Zoe had increased the gap between them to a full fifteen inches. It might as well have been a mile. Cooper was fast losing any semblance of optimism.

She'd let go of his hand a couple of properties back, using a particularly large seashell as an excuse. When she'd picked it up and they'd resumed walking, she hadn't noticed his outstretched hand. Or so she'd pretended.

"So," he said as they approached the beachside patio of the hotel.

There'd been a time when Zoe would've said "so" back, and they would've given each other a look, probably a goofy look if you asked anyone else, and they both would've laughed. Not tonight. Zoe didn't say a word now.

"Penn's party starts at seven tomorrow night." Cooper scrutinized her for any sign that he was misreading her but found nothing in her face that gave him hope.

"At the Shell Shack," she confirmed, glancing over her shoulder at another couple coming off the beach, looking much happier than Cooper and Zoe.

"We could go together," he risked. "Your mom too, of course."

"Mmm." She bit her lip and studied the white conch shell as it reflected the patio light. Her eyes closed tightly for a moment, and she shook her head. "Cooper, I can't do this."

He'd been half expecting the words or something similar, and still, the bottom dropped out of his gut. He swallowed back the swarm of emotion that suddenly tried to choke him. "Can't do what?" As if he didn't know. But he'd make her say it.

"This … *us*. There is no 'us'—"

"That's not what it seemed like half an hour ago."

She checked over her shoulder again, nervously this time, as if making sure there was no one to overhear her as she ripped out his heart. "That was a mistake, and you know it."

Hardening his heart, he went for flippant. "I'm a guy. Sex that amazing is never a mistake."

"It made everything more difficult. We aren't together. Aren't going to be together."

"We agreed to take what we could get for this weekend, Zo. That was more than I expected. So much better. Why ruin it with all this? Why not just get through the rest of the weekend and—"

"And then what, Cooper?" Steel lined her tone. "What's next? We waste another year traveling sixteen hundred miles once a month for some really good sex and to pretend like we have a real relationship with a real future?" Her jaw clamped down and she shook her head adamantly. "And every Monday morning, we have a painful reality check where it sets in that, once again, we're alone, and when you get down to it, we really have hardly anything without a future? I won't do that again. I *can't*."

"What if I considered moving to Colorado?" he said, feeling desperate at the thought of not seeing her again. Leaving San Amaro Island, the only place that had ever felt like home, was hard to imagine. He hated the idea.

After a moment's hesitation, Zoe surprised him by shaking her head fiercely. "I won't ask you to do that. I've never—"

"No. You didn't ask."

"Because I know what this place means to you, Cooper. If I made you choose between me and the home you love, who's to say you wouldn't end up resenting me?"

"Who's to say I would?"

"Would you have moved if I'd asked?" she said, finally meeting his eyes head on with hers.

He looked away, toward the waves, which, this far south, showed no sign of the otherworldly algae glow. He loved them anyway. Loved the gulf and the beach and the year-round decent weather, even the stifling-hot summer nights like this one.

"Your hesitation says it all, Cooper, and I can't hold that against you. Not when my answer was the same thing."

Not entirely the same, he thought to himself, as hers was a business decision more than love of the area she'd grown up in. But it didn't really matter, did it? What it came down to was the same dead end. The same losing proposition.

"Maybe I just need some time," he said, and without giving himself a chance to consider his action, he reached out and took her hand in his.

He saw Zoe swallow hard as her eyes lowered to their entwined hands. When she met his gaze again, tears made her eyes glisten in the low light.

"I'm sorry, Cooper. I love you." She hesitated and seemed to fight for control of herself, which tore him up even more. "I can't live in limbo anymore. I need either all of you or … none of you. I … I'm sorry."

She rose on her toes and planted a quick kiss on his lips, turned, and hurried away from him, into the refuge of the hotel lobby.

Cooper stared at the door where she'd disappeared, dumbfounded.

What the hell had just happened?

From the most amazing sex of his life to being walked out on in less than one hour?

He attempted to slam the brakes on the blinding pain that rolled over him and got the hell off the patio, where people milled around, probably staring at him, pitying his sorry ass.

He hurried away from the light from the buildings. Headed toward the escape the water offered. And when he got to the waves, he walked right goddamn into them, clothes, shoes, pain, and all.

10

Twelve hours and Zoe could blow this town. Ten and she would be at the airport, safely away from having to see Cooper again.

Every second of being in the same place with him, even if it was the sprawling, open-air patio of the Shell Shack beachside bar, made the hole in her chest stretch a little bigger.

She and Cooper had made peace on Thursday to avoid this kind of painful scene, but everything that had happened last night had screwed that up completely. Hopefully, Penn hadn't noticed the tension between them. He was so caught up in his eagerness to get to the witching hour, or in his case, the proposing hour, that he seemed to be floating around his birthday party only half-conscious of anything around him. Which was exactly how he should be.

"Hey! People!" The sound of Cooper's voice, yelling to be heard over the crowd of fifty or sixty people, made her nearly choke on the olive she'd just stuck in her mouth as she stood on the outskirts of a group of firefighters' wives she'd met several times on previous visits to the island. She followed the direction of it and spotted him on the opposite side of the patio, standing on top of one of the tables.

"Attention, you drunks!" he continued as the noise level

gradually lowered. "Listen up! The guest of honor here would like your attention."

This was it, Zoe knew, and she forced aside the ache inside of her to revel in her brother's big moment. Penn climbed up next to his roommate, and the two discussed something no one else could hear.

"Where's Nadia?" Cooper hollered, peering around the crowd.

A commotion near the thatched-roof shack that made up the bar proper indicated Nadia was over there.

"Nadia, your presence is requested. Stat!"

A wave of noise followed her across the patio to Cooper and Penn as she shot off remarks Zoe couldn't make quite make out. Wisecracks, no doubt. She'd fit in with the Griffin family just fine.

Nadia reached the table where Cooper and Penn towered over everyone. She stood in front of it, her neck craned upward as Penn tried to convince her to join him, and Cooper jumped down from the tabletop. Finally, Zoe's brother convinced Nadia that standing on top of a table in the middle of the bar was an okay thing to do this one time, and she climbed up. She looked fabulous up there in a royal blue skirt and top that looked like a one-piece dress, with a thin, lighter-blue belt and two-tone blue heels to die for. Her blond hair cascaded over her shoulders, shimmering in the bright security lights of the patio. Zoe searched the crowd for her mom, who she knew had agreed to record this moment on her phone. Spotting her about two tables away from Penn and Nadia, Zoe made her way next to her so she could see and hear better.

Nadia grinned and pushed her hair behind her ear self-consciously as she said something else Zoe couldn't hear.

"I'm embarrassing you?" Penn said without a drop of sympathy. "I'm just getting warmed up, my love." He took her hand and kissed the back of it in a sweet, old-fashioned move Zoe didn't know her brother had in him. Howls shot up from the partygoers, particularly the group of loud, hulking firefighters gathered in the corner of the patio.

Penn pulled Nadia to his side, his arm around her, as if to make her more comfortable.

"You all know that this incredible woman is behind this." He swung his unoccupied arm out to indicate the swarm of people on the patio. His grin was huge, and he took a moment to look around at everyone, shaking his head as if he couldn't believe so many people would show up to celebrate his birthday. "Thank you all for helping me turn thirty-three years old. I'm a little afraid of what she'll do when I hit a milestone like forty."

Peals of laughter and smartass comments rang out from the firefighters' corner.

"And thank you, Nadia, for this and everything you do for me." He angled her to face him as he got down to business. She shook her head modestly as if to say she didn't do that much.

"Oh, no you don't," Penn said, becoming serious. He took her hand again, and the crowd quieted and seemed to collectively lean forward to hear better. "I know you wanted to put me in the spotlight tonight, and I'll take that position, but not alone."

Nadia shook her head as she smiled. "Paybacks?"

Penn laughed. "Like you wouldn't believe, sweetheart. I have some things I want to say to you."

"Here?" she asked, glancing around at the crowd.

"Right here. In front of all these people who matter to me. I want everyone here to know how much you mean to me. Everyone who knows me knows the past two years have been a little slice of hell after my injury. I'm not a silent sufferer."

Nadia shook her head effusively, laughing.

"I made it through the toughest thing I've ever faced, and it's because of you. You were by my side, encouraging me from the start, long before I wanted to be encouraged, especially by the likes of this sexy woman who was everything good. I wasn't much in the mood for good back then."

"I kind of noticed," Nadia said, still grinning.

"I've got the best life I could ever hope for now, and it's a lot because of you."

The joking tone subsided as Penn clearly became overcome

with love for Nadia. Zoe wiped the tears that instantly welled up in her eyes.

"You helped me fight my way back to health when I just wanted to lie in bed and lash out. You helped me to step outside of my comfort zone. I thought I couldn't be happy unless I was a San Amaro Island firefighter, but I was so wrong. You encouraged me to look into becoming an arson investigator. Convinced me I could handle the classes and the training. Stood by my side as I made it through and took on a new career. You opened my eyes to embracing some hard changes, and I would do it all over again — every last bit — if it meant I'd end up with you."

Nadia dabbed at her eyes and pressed her lips together as if trying not to bawl. The tender look between them was so achingly bittersweet to Zoe that a tear or two fell down her cheeks as well. She silently cheered her brother on, the anticipation building to a peak.

Still holding Nadia's hand, Penn went down on one knee, right there on top of the table, and at once, Nadia covered her mouth with one hand and the crowd emitted a collective *aww*. He pulled the ring from his front pocket and held it out.

"Nadia, will you make me the happiest man alive and do me the honor of becoming my wife?"

COOPER HEADED toward the bar to buy his roommate a celebratory shot before he could do something stupid like get emotional. He was raw from last night, he reminded himself. As stoked as he was for Penn, the whole scene had gotten to him like he was some chick watching *Gone With the Wind* or something.

He himself had been around for the whole saga — Penn's back injury, Nadia's hovering, Penn's griping, and his entire recovery ordeal. He'd watched the two fall hard in spite of the circumstances. Couldn't be happier for his roomie, who'd had to fight through so much difficult shit to get his happiness.

It made his own current troubles seem like nothing.

As he approached the bar, part of Penn's speech — the part

about change and doing hard things — kept ringing through his head, nagging at him like an old woman. In an attempt to shut it down, he ordered three shots instead of two and downed the first right away.

The liquor didn't do a damn thing except maybe make it even clearer that he wanted exactly what Penn had found. And it didn't take a genius to figure out that Cooper had a chance to get it. The question was, did he have the balls to go for it?

11

FOUR WEEKS LATER

Eating dinner alone sucked, but it looked like Zoe would be doing it yet again tonight.

She shook the hot skillet to stir the chicken and veggies and prevent them from burning. Checking the clock on the stove, she wondered where the heck her mother was. She'd started cooking the second she'd gotten home from work so the food would be ready when her mom arrived and they could sit down to eat together for once. But so far, there was no sign of Nell.

She heard a vehicle out on the street, but it sounded like a big truck. Definitely not her mom's Lexus. At the slow squeal of powerful brakes right in front of their property, Zoe's curiosity was piqued. The kitchen was on the back of the house, so she went to the side window that overlooked the driveway to see if she could tell what was going on. The tail end of a local fire truck was barely visible. Her pulse kicked into overdrive. Was there a fire at one of their neighbors' houses?

A quick glance at the Barvinskys' house next door revealed nothing amiss, so she hurried into the living room for a better look at the rest of the neighborhood. And the truck.

Her alarm increased times one hundred when she realized

two firefighters in full gear, helmets and all, were heading up the walk to her front door. Her stir-fry hadn't even set off the smoke detector — she didn't need the fire department's help. She went to the door to tell them exactly that.

When she opened it, one of the men was already on the front steps, reaching toward the doorbell. The other stood several feet behind him. Perplexed, Zoe opened the screen door.

"Can I— Oh, my God." Her hand shot to her mouth as her mind tried to make sense of what her eyes took in.

Cooper had removed his helmet and gazed down at her with an expression in those blue eyes that she couldn't decipher. Zoe's gaze darted to his turnout coat with its Boulder Fire Department emblem on the chest.

"Hi, Zoe," he said with a measure of uncertainty.

"I don't… There's no… How did you get that coat?" she sputtered. She glanced behind him at the truck, which also proclaimed to be local. "What's going on, Cooper?"

"Please don't slam the door in my face," he said with a tone of conspiracy. "The guys are already giving me ten shades of hell."

"What are you doing here?" She looked from him to the man behind him, who she didn't recognize, to a group of four more fully outfitted firefighters lined up along this side of the truck, watching them.

"I moved to Colorado, Zo. These are my new co-workers." He gestured over his shoulder, then leaned forward to say, "They think I'm nuts."

Zoe nearly missed the last because her brain was still tripped up on the first. "You … *what*?" Was he kidding around?

That truck was real, though.

"You moved here?" she asked, not believing it but unable to come up with another explanation for the coat and the truck and the firefighters behind him.

"I got an apartment over on Crag View Road for now, short-term lease while I get my bearings. I've been with the department here for a week and a half."

She was sure her mouth gaped to her chest. "I don't understand."

"I'm here because of you, Zoe. Not because you asked me to or I felt obligated to. I chose to make this change on my own. Because I want that future you mentioned. I want to wake up beside you every single day."

He half turned and tossed his helmet the few feet to his closest ally. When he faced Zoe again, he rummaged around in the pocket of the large, thick coat, and then he went down on a knee, and Zoe's heart exploded in her chest.

"Cooper?" She pressed both her hands to her mouth, and her eyes teared up.

He held out a little black velvet box in one hand and took her hand in the other, drawing her completely out of the house and letting the screen door slam shut. "Zoe, I want to spend the rest of my life with you. Will you marry me?"

It was like time stopped for a second, like she was in some kind of a bubble of non-reality as she took in everything Cooper was saying, had said since she'd opened the door. His eyes, so full of love and tenderness. His calloused hands that held ... oh, holy hell, the most beautiful princess-cut diamond engagement ring in a platinum setting. What finally yanked her out of her stupor was the realization that his hand shook.

She met his eyes again and recognized the fear. Insecurity. Question.

She needed to fix that. As soon as her brain caught up.

"Y-you live here now?"

He nodded once, his eyes never veering from hers.

"You work for them?" She gestured to the truck.

"With them. Yes."

"What about your home? The island? Your condo?"

"I still have it. I'm going to rent it out to tourists when we're not there visiting. Zo? You're killing me."

She wasn't sure she understood the details, but she understood enough. He'd moved here. For her.

"Yes, Cooper," she finally said, the words spilling out on a stream of giddy laughter. "I'll marry you. Yes!"

He rose in a flash and picked her up in a bear hug, spinning her around. "Thank God," he mumbled. "You can't imagine what it took to get these guys to go along with this."

That was when she tuned in to the applause from the firefighters, the hoots and hollers and cheers, the calls of "way to go, Flannagan!"

Zoe, her feet still dangling above the ground, held on for dear life and breathed in the familiar smell of Cooper mixed with that of the stiff coat. She let it sink in that he was really here. In Colorado. With a ring.

"Let me see that thing," she said, lowering herself to the ground as best she could with Cooper's hold on her. "My ring. Please?"

Cooper laughed and steadied her, then took the ring out of the delicate box. He grasped her left hand and, his fingers still shaking, slid the ring onto her ring finger.

"I love it," she said, blinking away the tears that nearly blinded her. "It's perfect, Cooper." She turned her attention to his face. "I love you."

His laugh was a roar as he pulled her into his arms again. "I love you too, Zo Zo. I was going crazy without you."

"Me too," she said into his shoulder.

"If you'd said no, I would've never heard the end of it from my new colleagues. They think I'm batshit crazy as it is."

Zoe laughed. "You kind of are. In a good way. A very good way."

She opened her eyes finally, and that's when she noticed the beginnings of a crowd, attracted, no doubt, to the firetruck and trying to figure out what was going on. Her neighbors. The people she'd known for most of her life. And they were laughing and cheering along with the firefighters. She waved at them over Cooper's shoulder.

"Way to go, Zoe!" Mr. Finlay from down the block hollered, making her laugh again.

The firefighters who'd been by the truck were making their way to the porch to congratulate them.

"Nice work, Flannagan," the one who held Cooper's helmet

said as Cooper turned to face them all, pulling Zoe securely into his side.

"Told you she's a keeper," Cooper said as he shook their hands, one by one.

At that moment, an incessant beeping came from behind them, inside the house. Zoe recognized the sound in an instant.

"No! My dinner!" she said in alarm. She opened the door and could see a blanket of smoke near the ceiling, crawling its way into the living room from the kitchen. "I left my stir-fry cooking!"

She tried to run inside, but Cooper held on to her. "They've got it handled," he said, laughing, as three of the firefighters rushed inside her house.

"I just need to turn it off," she protested, slightly mortified that strangers had burst into her smoke-filled house.

"They've got it. You're staying right here with me. I'm not done with you yet," Cooper said with another gravelly laugh. She managed to forget about the alarm and the smoke as Cooper gazed into her eyes with so much love it just about knocked her over.

He pulled her close again and kissed her slowly, with such exquisite tenderness that she forgot where they were two seconds in. And then she registered the applause and the whistles and remembered they were in front of her house with a not-so-small audience. Laughing, she broke the contact of their lips and shook her head. "Enough. We're putting on a show."

Cooper laughed, too, and glanced over his shoulder at the gathering masses, who were coming closer. She expected him to lead her down the single step and out into the yard to meet them in the middle. Instead, he surprised her by spinning her into an old-fashioned dip and leaning over her to kiss her again.

Zoe let out what was embarrassingly close to a squeal at the suddenness of his big move and the fear that he might drop her. He held tightly though, and she gave in to the kiss for a few seconds.

"Okay," she said, laughing, trying to straighten but losing the battle. "You have to let me up. My kitchen's on fire, and my entire neighborhood is closing in on us."

"Zoe, my love, I just got you back. I don't care if the whole neighborhood burns down. I'm not letting you go."

He did, however, help her straighten. He tightened his arm around her waist as they both turned to her beloved neighbors, who were wishing them well. As she and Cooper went down the step toward them, she said, so only he could hear, "Is that a promise?"

"Biggest and best promise I ever made."

NOTE FROM THE AUTHOR

Thanks for reading *Fire Within, Impulse, and Slow Burn*! I hope you loved Nate and Sophie, Sawyer and Mariah, and Cooper and Zoe.

You might enjoy *True North*, the first book in my North Brothers series. See what happens when Mr. Socially Awkward spontaneously volunteers to be his beautiful boss's fake date.

"Amy Knupp has a way with writing that speaks to my heart. This book wasn't a home run to me. It was an all bases loaded grand slam!!!"—Reader Review for True North

These stories are part of the Island Fire series, which includes:

- Playing with Fire
- Heat of the Night
- Fully Involved
- Firestorm
- Afterburn
- Up in Flames
- Flash Point
- Fire Within
- Impulse
- Slow Burn

ALSO BY AMY KNUPP

<u>Henry Brothers Series</u>

Untold (prequel)

Unraveled

Unsung

Undone

<u>North Brothers Series</u>

True North

True Colors

True Blue

True Harmony

True Hero

North Brothers Box Sets:

North Brothers Books 1-3

North Brothers Books 4-5

North Brothers: The Complete Series

<u>Hale Street Series</u>:

Sweet Spot

Sweet Dreams

Soft Spot

One and Only

Last First Kiss

Heartstrings

<u>Hale Street Box Sets:</u>

Meet Me at Clayborne's

Clayborne's After Hours

It Happened on Hale Street

<u>Island Fire Series</u>:

Playing with Fire

Heat of the Night

Fully Involved

Firestorm

Afterburn

Up in Flames

Flash Point

Fire Within

Impulse

Slow Burn

Island Fire Box Sets:

Sparked (books 1-3)

Ignited (books 4-6)

Enflamed (books 7-10)

OR

Island Fire: The Complete Series

Themed Box Sets:

Friends to Forever (Friends to Lovers Romance)

Working It (Workplace Romance)

ABOUT THE AUTHOR

Amy Knupp is a *USA Today* Best-Selling Author of contemporary romance and a freelance copy editor. She loves words and grammar and meaty, engrossing stories with complex characters.

Amy lives in Wisconsin with her husband and has two sons, four cats, and a box turtle. She graduated from the University of Kansas with degrees in French and journalism. In her spare time, she enjoys traveling, breaking up cat fights, watching college hoops, and annoying her family by correcting their grammar.

For more information:
www.amyknuppbooks.com

To interact with Amy and other book lovers, please join her readers group, Books, Beaches, and Bellinis. If you'd like to know when her next book is available, you can sign up for her newsletter, follow her on BookBub and/or follow her on the social media below.